"You Want To Do *What?*"

"Desensitize you."

Considering the scandalized look on Ty's face, this was going to be a tougher sell than Tina anticipated. To make this work, he would have to relinquish control, and it was pretty clear that he thrived on being in control.

"I'm afraid to ask what that means," Ty said.

"In essence, you'll have to unlearn everything you've learned about sex and start over."

"And how would I do that?"

"Well, we would start with the basics, like holding hands. And when holding hands no longer makes you feel anxious, we move on."

His brow furrowed. She had his attention now. "Move on to what, exactly?"

"Well, sitting close. Kissing would probably be next." And boy, did Ty know how to kiss. Toe-curling, bone-melting, knock-your-socks-off-fantastic kisses.

"And then?"

"Touching."

He cleared h[...]ly will we be touchi[...]

She shrugged, and tried to keep her voice casual. "Eventually, everywhere."

Dear Reader,

This May, Silhouette Desire's sensational lineup starts with Nalini Singh's *Awaken the Senses*. This DYNASTIES: THE ASHTONS title is a tale of sexual awakening starring one seductive Frenchman. (Can you say ooh-la-la?) Also for your enjoyment this month is the launch of Maureen Child's trilogy. The THREE-WAY WAGER series focuses on the Reilly brothers, triplets who bet each other they can stay celibate for ninety days. But wait until brother number one is reunited with *The Tempting Mrs. Reilly*.

Susan Crosby's BEHIND CLOSED DOORS series continues with *Heart of the Raven,* a gothic-toned story of a man whose self-imposed seclusion has cut him off from love…until a sultry woman, and a beautiful baby, open up his heart. Brenda Jackson is back this month with a new Westmoreland story, in *Jared's Counterfeit Fiancée,* the tale of a fake engagement that leads to real passion. Don't miss Cathleen Galitz's *Only Skin Deep,* a delightful transformation story in which a shy girl finally falls into bed with the man she's always dreamed about. And rounding out the month is *Bedroom Secrets* by Michelle Celmer, featuring a hero to die for.

Thanks for choosing Silhouette Desire, where we strive to bring you the best in smart, sensual romances. And in the months to come look for a new installment of our TEXAS CATTLEMAN'S CLUB continuity and a brand-new TANNERS OF TEXAS title from the incomparable Peggy Moreland.

Happy reading!

Melissa Jeglinski

Melissa Jeglinski
Senior Editor
Silhouette Books

Please address questions and book requests to:
Silhouette Reader Service
U.S.: 3010 Walden Ave., P.O. Box 1325, Buffalo, NY 14269
Canadian: P.O. Box 609, Fort Erie, Ont. L2A 5X3

Bedroom Secrets

MICHELLE CELMER

Published by Silhouette Books

America's Publisher of Contemporary Romance

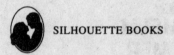 **SILHOUETTE BOOKS**

ISBN 0-373-76656-4

BEDROOM SECRETS

Copyright © 2005 by Michelle Celmer

This edition published by arrangement with Harlequin Books S.A.

® and TM are trademarks of Harlequin Books S.A., used under license.
Trademarks indicated with ® are registered in the United States Patent
and Trademark Office, the Canadian Trade Marks Office and in other
countries.

Visit Silhouette Books at www.eHarlequin.com

Printed in U.S.A.

Books by Michelle Celmer

Silhouette Desire

Playing by the Baby Rules #1566
The Seduction Request #1626
Bedroom Secrets #1656

Silhouette Intimate Moments

Running on Empty #1343

MICHELLE CELMER

lives in southeastern Michigan with her husband, their three children, two dogs and two cats. When she's not writing or busy being a mom, you can find her in the garden or curled up with a romance novel. And if you twist her arm real hard you can usually persuade her into a day of power shopping.

Michelle loves to hear from readers. Visit her Web site at: www.michellecelmer.com, or write her at P.O. Box 300, Clawson, MI 48017.

To my great-nephews, Thomas Zachary
and Connor Michael. Welcome to the world, guys.

One

She didn't have enough money.

Tina DeLuca studied the change in her hand, dread creeping in to seize the empty space in her stomach the measly bowl of soup hadn't filled. It had been the cheapest thing on the menu with any nutritional value. What she hadn't counted on was the sales tax.

Not only did she not have money for the check, she wouldn't have enough to use the pay phone on the off chance that she'd found her father. She'd hoped to call first rather than just showing up on his doorstep. Then she could at least determine if he was the correct Martin Lopez before she went barging in on his life.

And if he wasn't? If this was another dead end? That feeling of dread swept back in. She was out of money with not a soul on earth to call for help. She had reached the end of the line. She could only hope the city had some sort of shelter she could spend the night in.

Or a jail, which is exactly where she would wind up if she couldn't pay her bill, or somehow con her way out of paying it. But the only thing she hated more than being homeless and penniless was lying.

"Wherever God closes a door he opens a window," her mother had written in her journal. Which had Tina wondering if the restroom had a window she could slip through.

No. She'd come this far without lying or cheating anyone. She would just have to be honest and hope the kind-faced woman took pity on her.

"You sure I can't get you anything else, hon?" The kindly old waitress she suspected was the "Mae" of Mae's Diner hovered by her table and Tina's heart began to pound. Her hands shook so badly some of the change she'd been holding dropped and scattered across the table.

Mae's face went from mildly confused to downright concerned. "Are you okay?"

Tina felt like the world's biggest phony. How could she look this thoughtful woman in the eye and tell her that not only was she not going to get a tip for her exemplary service, she was going to be shortchanged on the check.

Tina had to come clean.

Her nearly empty stomach pitched and rolled, and she felt light-headed. Just do it.

"I don't have enough," she said, but it came out so softly and her voice was quivering so badly that Mae didn't understand her.

"What was that, hon? You don't what?"

"Have enough money," she said more loudly, and the two women seated in the next booth turned to look at her with unmasked distaste. Tina's face burned with shame. Could this be any more humiliating? "I thought I would have enough," she explained. "But I forgot the sales tax. I'm twenty cents short."

Mae lifted one penciled-in brow. "Twenty cents, huh?"

Tina felt tears welling in her eyes and fought to hold them in. This wasn't the time to throw herself a pity party. She didn't want Mae to think she was some kind of con artist. "I'll do dishes," she said. "Or I can cook. I'm a great cook."

Mae frowned. "You're not from around here, are you?"

Tina shook her head.

"Come with me." Mae stepped aside so Tina could get out of her seat. Then she added, "To my office."

This is it, Tina thought, her heart sinking so low she could feel the persistent throb of her pulse all the way down to her toes. Mae was going to call the police. Oh well, a jail cell was better than sleeping on the street. And if Ray reported what had happened last week, there was no doubt she would be arrested—for assault.

Tina stood on wobbly legs and grabbed her backpack from the bench seat. Holding her head high despite the look of pure disdain from the women in the next booth, she followed Mae to the front of the restaurant. She tried to see herself through their eyes. Her clothes were rumpled and dirty from several days without seeing the inside of a washing machine. She probably looked like one of the homeless people she'd seen sleeping at the bus station. She *was* homeless.

Mae led her through the busy kitchen, and Tina's stomach rumbled from all of the magnificent smells lingering there. It had been days since she'd had a real meal. To stretch her limited funds she'd existed on a meager diet, one that consisted primarily of soup and crackers.

Mae led her into a tiny office near the back and gestured to one of the metal chairs opposite a small cluttered desk. "What's your name, hon?"

"Tina," she said, lowering herself into the chair closest to her and resting her bag against her legs. "Tina DeLuca."

"Well, Tina DeLuca, you wait here." Mae left, closing the door behind her and Tina steeled herself for what was to come. She looked up at several decades' worth of Chamber of Commerce awards and a poster boasting Mae's pastries to be the best in Michigan. Dozens of framed photos of what must have been Mae's children and grandchildren lined the wall. Everyone looked so happy.

A big, happy family. Tina was a stranger to the concept. After she'd lost her mother, it had been only her, Aunt Louise and cousin Ray.

Some day I'll have a real family, she thought. She would find the right man, settle down and have lots of babies. If she was patient, it would happen.

After she got out of prison.

She leaned her head back against the wall and closed her eyes. Lord, she was exhausted. She hadn't slept more than a few hours a night since she'd left Philadelphia. She wondered if the beds in jail were more comfortable than a bus seat.

The door opened and a ripple of fear turned her limbs to jelly. She waited for the inevitable. For Mae to tell her the police were on the way.

Instead the woman set a plate down on the desk in front of Tina. A plate piled high with French fries and an enormous cheeseburger. Next to it she set a large glass of soda.

Mouth gaping, all Tina could do was stare. Why was Mae bringing her more food when she couldn't even pay for her soup?

Mae circled the desk and took a seat, sliding the top drawer open. She rifled through it for a moment, then looked up at Tina, her brow raised. "Are you just going to stare at it?"

"But…"

"You're hungry, aren't you?"

Mae wasn't calling the police. She was going to help her. Tina's fear melted away and tears welled in her eyes. She hadn't known such kindness existed anymore.

"Is there someone I can call for you, hon?"

Tina shook her head. "There's no one."

"I didn't think so. Go ahead and eat it while it's hot." She returned her attention to the open drawer. "Now, I know that card is in here somewhere."

Tina picked up a French fry and bit off a piece. It was greasy and salty and the most heavenly thing she'd ever tasted, and she could hardly swallow past the lump of emotion in her throat.

"Ah, here it is." Mae pulled a slightly worn business card from the drawer and slid it across the desk.

Tina picked it up and read the name—Tyler Douglas. There was no title. Just an address and phone number.

"My sister, bless her decrepit soul, has worked for Tyler for years cleaning his rental properties. Well, her sciatica has gotten pretty bad this past year, and she can't manage all the bending and stretching anymore.

Especially in the cold weather. Just yesterday she told Tyler she had to quit, so I know for a fact he's looking for someone to fill the position."

When God closes a door he opens a window.

"A job?" Tina asked.

"You tell him Mae sent you over and he'll set you up." Mae stood, smoothing the front of her uniform. "You go ahead and finish your lunch, then you can let yourself out the back door."

"Thank you. I'll pay you for the food as soon as I can," Tina assured her.

Mae just smiled. "I know you will."

As Mae disappeared through the door, Tina could swear she saw the hint of a halo just above the woman's silvery hair. And somewhere in the back of her mind she could hear the faintest sound of a window sliding open.

Tyler Douglas was putting his foot down.

Emily was his sister, and he loved her, but he had to draw the line at this. "There is no way in hell I'm standing up in your wedding with a guy."

"But you're the best man and Alex is my best friend," Emily said, as if it was a completely logical deduction. "You *have* to stand up together."

"Alex is *gay*."

There was a pause then, "So?"

"What do you mean, *so?* What if people think we're…together?"

"Alex was right—you are homophobic."

"I wouldn't walk down the aisle with *any* guy: gay, straight or undecided. And what does Mom think about you having a man for a maid of honor?" When she didn't answer, he laughed. "You haven't told her yet, have you?"

"It doesn't matter what Mom thinks. It's my wedding."

"Yeah, you keep telling yourself that."

"Just think about it, okay? Hey, and while I've got you on the phone, Matt said there's a new secretary at the high school. Blond, big breasts, shallow—just the way you like 'em."

"You're not winning any points here."

"I'm just kidding. Matt said she's very nice. And single. We could double."

"No, thanks."

"Are you going through some kind of romantic dry spell or something?"

Her question hit home like a dynamite blast, making him wince. *Dry spell* didn't begin to describe it. But things would get better. In time, he would be back to his old virile self.

He hoped.

"You know," Emily said, "if there's something wrong, you can talk to me about it."

"There's nothing wrong." Nothing a few years of intense psychotherapy wouldn't cure. No way in hell he could talk to his sister about *that*.

"Ty, since middle school you've *always* had a girlfriend. Sometimes two or three at a time."

The outer office door jingled and he silently thanked whoever it was for the interruption. "Hey, someone's here. Gotta run. I'll call you later."

"Ty—"

"Say hi to Matt for me. Love you." He hit the disconnect button and set the phone down. That was a close call, and knowing Emily, he hadn't heard the last of this. Though they weren't identical, they were still bound by that cosmic connection twins often have. Depending on the circumstances, that could be a good or a bad thing.

"Hello?" a voice called from the lobby.

A female voice. Damn.

"In here," Ty called back. He really needed to get a new receptionist to screen his visitors. Preferably an ugly receptionist. Or better yet, a man.

The source of the voice, who appeared in his office a second later, was neither ugly nor male. One look at her dark, inquisitive eyes, flawlessly smooth olive skin, and he instinctively took a step to the left, behind the safety of his desk.

Damn, it was really getting out of control when he couldn't be in the same room with a beautiful woman without running for cover. Three months ago, he would have met her by the door and taken her hand, simply for the pleasure of testing the softness of her skin. There was a time when he'd loved everything about women. The way they smelled, the way they tasted, the silky softness of their hair.

Now he viewed them as the enemy. And he knew with no small measure of certainty, this woman could push all the right buttons if he let her.

"Are you Tyler Douglas?" she asked.

He pasted on a charming smile. "The one and only. What can I do for you?" Please let it be something quick and painless.

She returned the smile times ten. "Mae sent me over. She said you're looking for a cleaning lady."

Oh man, was she beautiful. And so young. He felt like a degenerate for the thoughts tumbling through his depraved brain. Things like the fullness of her breasts cupped into his palms, her slender fingers tunneling through his hair as he plundered her lush mouth with passionate kisses. She would taste sweet and tangy and…and oh man, he needed to stop this right now or he would be sorry. He could already feel the shift in his breathing, the familiar tug in his groin.

She stepped closer and his pulse began to accelerate. A cold sweat broke out across his forehead and his head began to spin.

Relax. Breathe, in and out.

"My name is Tina DeLuca," she said, holding out a hand for him to shake. He dreaded the words he knew were coming next. "I'd like the job."

Two

Brad Pitt, eat your heart out, Tina thought as she tried her best not to stare. They sure knew how to grow them in Chapel, Michigan. For some reason she'd been expecting someone older. Someone not so strikingly handsome or built to complete physical perfection.

Someone who wouldn't look at her as if…she was a leper.

He retreated a step and waved away her extended hand. "We don't stand on formality here," he said.

Oookay.

She let her arm fall to her side. Not quite sure what to do with her hands, she clasped them behind her back. She'd never gone on a job interview before and wasn't sure of the proper etiquette. Since the time she was old enough to have a real job, she'd been taking care of Aunt Louise. Her people skills were a tad rusty.

"Is the position still open?" she asked.

"Yes, but uh, the pay is pretty low."

It couldn't be any lower than the nothing she was currently earning. "That's okay."

"I mean really low, like minimum wage."

"Minimum wage works for me."

He frowned, his blond brow dipping low over his eyes. "It's really lousy work."

She tried to keep her voice cheerful when inside her heart was plummeting. Mae had made this sound like a sure thing. If she didn't get this job, she wasn't sure what she would do. Where she would go. She had no place to stay, no place to sleep. "I like to clean. And I have a lot of experience," she added.

"A pretty girl like you? Wouldn't you be happier as a model or something?"

A *model?* Was he kidding? At five foot two and 111 pounds, she wasn't exactly runway material. "Mr. Douglas—"

"Ty," he said, then winced, as though revealing his name had been some sort of fatal error. "Everyone around here calls me Ty."

"Ty, I'm a hard worker."

"I'm sure you are, Miss…?"

"Where I'm from, people call me Tina."

"I don't doubt that you are, Tina. I'm just not sure it would be a very good idea."

He wasn't going to hire her. She could tell by the look on his face. He was going to tell her no.

In the back of her mind she could hear the window again, but this time it was slamming shut. All she could do now was stick her fingers in the way and hope they weren't lobbed off.

She took a deep breath, gathering all her courage, but still her voice shook when she spoke. "I really need this job. I'm desperate."

"I understand." He shrugged sympathetically. "I wish I could help you."

The last bit of strength she'd been clinging to crumbled away, and the dam on her emotions broke. She was so tired of being lonely and afraid and hungry. She was just plain tired.

And she couldn't be strong another minute. She crumpled into a chair, dropped her face in her hands and started to cry.

Aw, man, he'd made her cry. Ty looked helplessly around, wondering what he should do now. Seeing her bawling, knowing it was his fault, was even worse than the dizziness and the cold sweats.

Well, maybe not worse, but almost as bad. And it could have been avoided if he wasn't so selfish. He hated what was happening to him, but he didn't have a clue how to stop it—to fix it. His original plan—ignore it until it goes away—didn't seem to be working very well.

And now, not only was *he* miserable, he was dragging other people down with him.

He grabbed a tissue and leaned over his desk to press it into her hand. "Here."

She took it, wiped her eyes and nose. "I'm sorry," she said. "I didn't mean to fall apart. It's been a really bad week."

"I can relate," he said. More than once in the past three months he'd felt like sitting down and bawling, too.

"Just give me a minute to pull myself together and I'll be out of your hair." As she wiped away fresh tears, he realized there was no makeup on her face to smear. No mascara running down her cheeks. Hers was a natural beauty. Her face didn't get all blotchy and red when she cried either like a lot of women he'd known. She might have looked wholesome had her dark features not been so exotic.

But she was just a kid. He was guessing no more than sixteen or seventeen. And she must have needed the job pretty badly to get this upset. She looked so lost. So... *helpless.*

Aw, *hell.*

"Can you start tomorrow morning?"

She looked up at him, lower lip still quivering. "You'll hire me?"

She had trouble written all over her. But could he help that he was a sucker for a woman in distress? He knew it was a huge mistake. But it wouldn't be his first, or his last.

Ignore it until it goes away.

Yeah, right.

He jotted an address on a slip of paper and located the correct key from the top drawer of his desk. He handed them both to her. "Everything you need is at the house. Cleaning supplies, vacuum, mop. The painters finished up two days ago, so everything should be dry by now."

"I'm doing the entire house?"

"Top to bottom. Is that a problem?"

She shook her head. "No. No problem at all."

"I want to start showing the property to renters as soon as possible, so try to get it done tomorrow if you can. When you're done, I'll come inspect it, and if everything looks good, I'll cut you a check. If it works out,

I have a small office building one block over I'll need done later this week."

She was actually smiling now. A brilliant smile that lit her whole face and warmed him from the outside in. He liked too much that he could make her that happy so easily. It shouldn't have mattered how she felt.

At least he seemed to be over his initial anxiety. As long as he didn't get too close to her he should be okay. But man, she was pretty. And vulnerable.

What the hell was he doing?

"Thank you Mr.—I mean, Ty. Thank you so much for giving me a chance. You won't be sorry."

He almost laughed. He was sorry already.

Tina gazed up at the brick bungalow that matched the address on the slip of paper Ty had given her. It had taken her a long time to find it in the unfamiliar city. So long it was already growing dark. Icy wind whipped around her, penetrating her denim pants and thin nylon jacket and sending leaves scurrying down the street. She was cold and exhausted and ached for a restful night of sleep. And a hot shower would be heaven. She hadn't showered in days, only cleaned herself up as best as a person could in a bus station restroom. Which wasn't all that great. Her skin felt grimy and her hair dirty and her scalp was itching like crazy.

She couldn't believe what she was considering doing.

It wasn't exactly breaking and entering, because she had a key. And it would be for only one night. Tomorrow she would have money for a motel. And a meal. And, of course, she would go back to the diner and pay Mae. If it wasn't for the kind old woman, Tina wouldn't have a place to sleep tonight. Or food in her belly.

And Tyler, well, she hadn't quite figured him out yet. If she didn't know any better, she would think he was afraid of her. Which didn't make any sense at all. A man so physically beautiful couldn't possibly be insecure. Everything about him screamed all-American hero.

Lord knows, he was her hero.

And how would he feel if he knew she was seriously thinking about crashing in his rental house? She would be violating his trust.

Well, not exactly, because technically he never said she *couldn't* sleep here tonight. And what he didn't know wouldn't hurt him. Right? This way, she could get an early start on the cleaning and have it done in plenty of time. Then he would be more likely to give her another building to clean.

She had to make up her mind soon, or people would start to notice her standing there and get suspicious.

Sleep on the street in a box somewhere in the freezing cold, or in a warm house? Wow. That was a tough one. She took the key from her pocket and started up the cement walk to the front door.

Before she could talk herself out of it, she'd slipped the key into the lock, turned the knob, opened the door and stepped inside.

The room smelled of latex paint and new carpet and the air was chilly. With the blinds closed, it was dark, so she felt along the wall where she thought the light switches might be until she found one. She blinked against the sudden bright light and looked around. Beige walls, beige carpet. Small, but cute. It was so clean, she wondered what it was she was expected to do. But when she looked more closely she noticed the blinds were coated with a thick layer of greasy dust. She suspected the windows could use a good polishing.

No problem.

An archway to the right led into a tiny kitchen and nook. In the corner sat all the supplies she would need. Cleaning solvents, buckets, rolls of paper towels and scrub brushes.

The floor in here definitely needed a thorough scrubbing and a coat of wax. The stove was crusted with baked-on food and grease. She pulled the fridge open and the rank odor seeping out nearly singed the skin off her face. Eew!

She slammed the door shut. That would need a major disinfecting and some serious airing-out.

Her bladder full to bursting, she decided her next stop would be the bathroom. She found it down the hall, next to two small bedrooms. Thank goodness, someone had left toilet paper on the roll and a bar of soap by the sink. But the room reeked of mildew. She pulled back the shower curtain and immediately realized why. Halfway up the tile wall the grout was black with it. She definitely had her work cut out for her. But she hadn't been exaggerating when she'd told Ty she liked cleaning. As cooking and caring for her aunt had, it gave her tremendous satisfaction.

Her cousin Ray had wanted her to take care of him, too. In an altogether different way, she thought with a shudder of disgust. She wondered how long he'd spent sprawled and unconscious on the kitchen floor. And what his reaction had been when he'd realized she was gone. The memory of his meaty hands groping her, his rank breath on her face, turned her stomach.

That was all behind her now. She would find her father and start a new life somewhere. Maybe right here in Chapel.

She found the thermostat and cranked the heat up to a balmy seventy-five degrees. By the time she finished showering it was warm enough in the house to walk around in only a T-shirt. She threw what few clothes she had in the washing machine in the basement and settled into one of the bedrooms. She shut the light off and, using her backpack as a pillow, stretched out on the carpet. Her entire body sighed with fatigue. She couldn't have lain there for more than five minutes before she was sound asleep.

Until she heard something.

She bolted upright, heart pounding, disoriented in the dark. She wasn't even sure what had woken her, but she knew something wasn't right. After years of caring for her elderly aunt, she'd trained herself to sleep lightly, to wake at the slightest hint of trouble, the faintest sound. She groped for the watch hooked on her backpack and lit the tiny face. Almost midnight. Then she heard it again. Footsteps.

Someone was in the house.

For a second she was frozen with fear, then instinct snapped in and she scrambled up, grabbed her backpack and headed for the closet. She pulled the door closed and it shut with a loud snap. She cursed silently, hoping the intruder hadn't heard. It wouldn't take them long to realize the house was empty and there was nothing to steal. Unless stealing wasn't what they had in mind. Maybe someone had seen her enter earlier and knew she was here alone and defenseless. Had she even locked the door before she'd fallen asleep?

Heart sinking, hands trembling, she dug through the

pack for her pepper spray. She closed her fingers around the small canister and flattened herself against the back wall. Through the cracks around the door, she could see the light come on and her heart seized, then restarted triple-time. She stood frozen with fear, finger on the trigger, ready to fire. The footsteps were closer, and a shadow fell over the door, then the door swung open—

Tina closed her eyes tight and shoved her finger down on the trigger, letting the pepper spray rip.

"Son of a—!"

Uh-oh. She recognized that voice.

She opened her eyes and the pepper spray dropped from her hand.

Spitting out a stream of curses, Tyler Douglas stood in the middle of the room wrestling a black leather jacket off his arms. He flung it to the carpet and clawed at his shirt. Buttons flew in all directions as he ripped it open and tore it off. The skin underneath was beet-red. That's when she realized she must have sprayed him not in the face, but in the chest. Not surprising, considering he was at least a foot taller than her and she'd never thought to aim up.

"Damn, that burns," he groaned.

She could see he was in agony, and snapped out of her shocked state when she saw him lifting his hands to his eyes. "Don't touch your face! It's pepper spray."

"Pepper spray? What the hell—"

"The bathroom," she said, leaping from the closet and grabbing his arm. "We have to wash it off you!"

She dragged him down the hall to the bathroom. Flinging back the shower curtain, she turned the cold water on full-blast and shoved him under it—clothes and all.

Ty gasped as the icy water nailed him in the chest, but at least it eased the burning sensation on his skin and the constricting ache in his lungs. His eyes were beginning to burn so he stuck his face under, too, filling his mouth with water and spitting it back out. He'd never been sprayed before, but he knew the logical thing to do was to wash as much of it off as possible.

When he looked out at Tina, she was staring at her hands, eyes wide, the color leached from her face. "It burns."

Aw, hell. He grabbed her arm and pulled her into the tub with him. When the first blast of cold water hit her she squealed and tried to break free, but he held on. He hugged her against his chest, tucking her head snugly under his chin. "Hold still."

"Cold," she gasped.

No kidding. He was soaked to the bone and shivering, but it sure as hell beat that agonizing burn. If he wasn't so concerned about her welfare, he'd be ripping her a new one right now.

She stopped struggling and went very still in his arms. A moment later she said softly, "I feel better. You think maybe you could, um, let me go now?"

He looked down and realized his hand was cupped over her generous left breast. He abruptly let go and backed away from her. How in the hell had he gone from not being able to be in the same room with Tina, to groping her in the shower?

Excruciating pain maybe?

She bent over and shut the water off, then turned to face him. Her dark hair hung in damp ringlets around her face. Her T-shirt was dripping and hung heavy against her full breasts, outlining everything down to the finest detail, and considering the frigid water temperature, there was *a lot* of detail. And hey, she wasn't wearing pants. Could this get any better?

At least she was wearing panties—skimpy pink panties with what looked like kittens on them. *Jesus.*

She looked damned appealing standing there. So why wasn't his heart racing? Why wasn't he sweating and short of breath?

Because he was blood-boiling, spitting mad, he realized. Despite the fact that he had a near-naked, soaking-wet, sexy-as-hell woman less than three feet away, this was the least arousing situation he'd been in his whole damned life.

Hallelujah, he was cured.

"I am so sorry," she said, her lower lip trembling. It could have been from the cold, or fear. Frankly he didn't care which.

He wiped away the water that was leaking off his hair and dripping into his eyes. "Is that so?"

"I can explain everything."

"Good. Explain to me what the hell you're doing in my house."

Three

"C-could I dry off f-first?" Tina asked, her voice quivering. Not only were her lips trembling, they were turning blue.

"Yeah, sorry." Ty stepped out of the tub, his tennis shoes squishing on the tile. He was pretty cold himself. But when he looked around for something to dry off with, he remembered the house was empty. There were no towels.

Great.

"P-paper towels in the kitchen," she said, hugging herself.

Better than nothing.

His shoes making a loud sucking noise against his feet, he walked out to the kitchen and grabbed two rolls. Back in the bathroom he ripped one package open and tossed it to her, then opened the other for himself.

He pulled a handful of towels loose and dried his chest and arms. "Where are your clothes?" he asked.

She bit her lip. "In the washing machine."

He closed his eyes and cursed under his breath. "Tell me they're not wet."

"They're wet. I was going to put them in the dryer but I forgot."

"Wonderful. You don't have *anything* that's dry?"

She shook her head.

"I have a gym bag in my truck. There's probably something in there you could wear. While I'm getting it, do me a favor and put your clothes in the dryer. Okay?"

She nodded.

He left her in the bathroom and trudged out the front door, bare-chested and soaking wet, into the near-freezing air. When he'd driven past on his way home and seen the kitchen light blazing, he'd figured the painters or carpet installers had left it on. Never had he expected to find Tina hiding in the bedroom closet.

And he really hadn't expected to be blasted with pepper spray.

He grabbed his gym bag off the front seat of his truck and jogged back up to the house. No way was he getting her out of here without dry clothes on. It was far too cold. She'd end up with pneumonia.

When he stepped back inside she was just emerging from the basement. He dropped the bag on the floor and dug through it until he found what he was looking for.

"I turned the heat up," she said.

He handed her a T-shirt and drawstring running shorts. "Put these on."

Tina looked at the clothes he'd handed her, then back at him. He was just as wet as she was, and that soaked denim couldn't have been very comfortable. "What about you?"

"Boxers," he said, holding up a plaid pair. Her surprise must have shown because he narrowed his eyes at her and said, "Is that a problem?"

"Nope." She was just grateful he hadn't tossed her out on her ear. Although, she was sure that was next. No way he would let her keep her job now.

And who was she to complain if he wanted to walk around in his underwear? She'd imagined what he might look like without his clothes on. How could she not? She'd just never thought she would ever see him that way. And so far she wasn't disappointed. She could swear his shoulders were about a yard wide, and his pecs were downright enormous. He was big all over, but not an ounce of him appeared to be fat.

"I'm going to go downstairs and change and throw my pants in the dryer, then we're going to have a talk about your future employment."

In other words, there would be no future employment. She nodded and he disappeared down the stairs.

How had she managed to screw things up so badly? She could try crying again, but she doubted even that would work. Besides, she'd never been the type who could whip up fake tears on cue.

She locked herself in the bathroom and peeled off her wet clothes. The things Ty had given her were way too big, but they were dry and would keep her modestly covered until her clothes were out of the dryer.

She still couldn't believe they'd stood in the shower together, semi-naked, and he'd had his hand on her breast. With the exception of her gynecological exam last year, she hadn't been touched there since the summer before her senior year of high school, when she'd gone parking with Joe DeCaussin. He'd wanted to go farther, but she wouldn't let him. She'd told him, next time, not knowing there wouldn't be a next time.

Aunt Louise had had her second stroke the very next day, effectively putting an end to Tina's social life.

Of course there was cousin Ray. He'd touched her breast, but that didn't count since it had been revolting and against her will.

But Ty's hand had felt really nice resting there, after her hands and eyes had stopped burning.

She hung her wet T-shirt over the curtain rod to dry and used paper towels to mop up the puddles of water on the floor.

She noticed the mildew again and wondered if there was bleach with the cleaning supplies in the kitchen. Then she remembered it wasn't her problem to deal with any longer. She was once again out of a job and homeless with no one to turn to for help. She should have been scared to death, but for some reason she just felt numb. Maybe she could curl up, go to sleep and when she woke, everything would be okay again.

She heard Ty's heavy footsteps on the basement stairs and, knowing she should just get this over with, opened the bathroom door and walked out into the living room where he was—oh boy—wearing nothing but boxer shorts. His legs were thick with corded muscle and covered with sandy-colored hair. She'd never seen a man this naked this close up before.

"They fit okay?" Ty asked, gesturing to the clothes he'd given her.

"Yes, thank you."

"You may as well get comfortable," he said.

He sat on the carpet, his back against the wall, so she sat a few feet away against the adjacent wall, tucking her knees up under her chin.

"So," he said, "why did you feel it was necessary to douse me with pepper spray?" He said it so calmly, when he must have been furious with her.

"I didn't know it was you. I thought it was an intruder."

"I own the house. *You* were the intruder."

"I know. I'm sorry. I made a mistake."

"Which brings me to my next question. What were you doing half-naked in my house in the first place? And don't tell me cleaning."

"I was sleeping. I needed a place to stay."

Anger leaked into his voice. "So you never really wanted the job? You just needed a place to crash?"

"No! I did need the job. I *do* need it."

"You said you know Mae. Was that a lie, too?"

"Of course not! I met her at the diner. She gave me your business card when—" she paused, still humiliated by the experience.

"When what?"

"When I couldn't pay my bill. I forgot about the sales tax and was twenty cents short. She took me into her office and I thought she was going to call the police."

"The police? For twenty cents? You're not from around here are you?"

She shook her head. "Instead she brought me a hamburger and gave me your card."

"Mae has a big heart."

She nodded again, emotion catching in her throat.

He cringed. "You're not going to cry again, are you?"

She swallowed hard and shook her head.

"I'm going to ask you a question and I want an honest answer, okay?"

"Okay."

"Did you run away from home?"

"Sort of, I guess."

He sighed and dragged a hand across his face. "Then we need to call your parents. They're probably worried sick about you."

He thought she was a *teenage* runaway? She nearly laughed. Did she really look *that* young? "Sorry, but that's impossible."

"No matter how bad things are, running away isn't the answer. And I can get in a lot of trouble letting you stay here."

"I doubt that." At least not for the reason he was thinking. Harboring a fugitive maybe.

"I'm sure you've heard of statutory rape. I'm twenty-eight years old, and you're what? Sixteen, seventeen?"

"Twenty-one."

He lifted a skeptical brow. "Uh-huh. Sure you are."

"Seriously, I am. My driver's license is in my backpack in the bedroom closet. Go get it if you don't believe me."

He made no move to get up. "If you're twenty-one, why did you run away from home?"

"I didn't have a choice. It wasn't *my* home anymore. My aunt died and my cousin…kicked me out. I have no money, no home and no family. And no, that's not a sob story to make you feel sorry for me. It just is what it is."

He was quiet for a minute, then he said, "What about your parents?"

"My mother died a long time ago and I never knew

my father. I've been trying to find him, and I traced him to Chapel. That's why I'm here."

"But you don't have any money?"

She shook her head, because it was too humiliating to say out loud.

"And how long ago did your cousin kick you out?"

"Five days. I figured I would have found my father by now and he could help me. But all I've found are a bunch of dead ends."

"Why should I believe anything you say?"

"I guess you don't have to. But if you have any compassion at all you won't fire me. I need to pay Mae back and find my father. I *need* the job."

He sighed again, rubbing his red-rimmed eyes. "I should boot you out on your behind, but for some reason I actually believe you, so I'll let you keep the job. But only if you promise to be nice to me from now on."

She froze and bile crept up her throat. No way. This couldn't be happening to her again. And to think she'd trusted him. Would he try to force himself on her like Ray had, or did he just expect her to lie back and let it happen?

When she sprayed him earlier she should have run. She should have gotten out when she could. And now here they were, her in his clothes and him in his underwear. Why hadn't she seen this coming? How could she be so foolish?

Ty leaned forward, as if he was going to get up, and Tina scrambled to the corner of the room, as far from him as she could get. "Don't touch me!"

He looked up, surprised. "What?"

"I'll leave as soon as my clothes are dry, just stay away from me."

"Tina, what are you talking about? I said you could have the job."

"I don't care how bad I need it. I'm not having sex with you."

He blinked, looking impossibly confused. "When did I ask you to have sex with me?"

She frowned. Why did he not seem to know what the heck she was talking about? "You said I had to be nice to you. I thought…"

"I meant nice like, you won't attack me with your pepper spray again. Why would you think sex would be part of the bargain? I mean, besides the obvious, that I'm sitting here in my skivvies and I accidentally grabbed your breast in the shower?"

She didn't answer. She couldn't. It was too humiliating. And she didn't even have to, he figured it out all by himself.

He cursed and shook his head. "Who was it? Don't tell me your cousin."

"He's a cousin by marriage. Not blood."

He tossed his hands up. "Well, that makes it so much less perverse."

"I should have seen it coming," she said. "He always was kind of creepy."

Ty said firmly, "Don't you dare tell me it was your fault. No one should have to *see* something like that coming. What were you doing living with a guy like that anyway?"

"I wasn't living with him. It was my aunt's house. My cousin Ray told me I would get the house and half my aunt's money when she passed away."

"But you didn't," Ty said. It was stated as a fact, not a question.

"It was all a lie. He never intended to give me a dime. But at least I had a roof over my head and food on the table. Then I found out that came with a condition."

"What kind of condition?"

"I had to be 'nice' to him."

"Sick bastard." Ty tunneled his fingers through his damp hair. He'd figured when she showed up in his office that she was pretty desperate for a job. He just hadn't realized *how* desperate.

And it occurred to him suddenly that he'd been sitting in the same room with her for a while now, in his underwear no less, and he hadn't once felt even a hint of anxiety. He still found her attractive, but he was feeling this brotherly protectiveness toward her that overshadowed any romantic feelings. "So, you think your father is here in Chapel?"

"I hope so."

"This is a pretty small city. Maybe I would recognize his name."

"Martin Lopez?"

"Doesn't sound familiar to me, but that doesn't mean he doesn't live here. I've got a P.I. I use for background checks. I could have him look into it."

Her eyes lit for a second, then the hope fizzled away. "I appreciate the offer, but I don't have money for that."

"I didn't ask you for money."

"I can't take charity from you."

"You were planning on staying in my house tonight, weren't you?"

"That's different. You were going to pay me to clean it. And it was that or sleep on the street."

"And what about tomorrow night and the next?"

"I was going to get a motel room."

"There's only one motel in walking distance and it's not exactly cheap."

She chewed on her lip. "I'll figure something out. Maybe I can find a shelter."

"Not in Chapel. This is a small city. We don't have the funding for that—or the need."

She began to wring her hands together and he could tell she was on the verge of panic.

"Tell you what," he said. "You can come home with me."

"With you?" she said warily.

If someone had told him yesterday that he would make her an offer like that he'd have laughed at them, but was it really such a bad idea? He could be in the same room with her and not hyperventilate. Maybe they could spend some time together and in doing so he could work through this anxiety thing. Maybe this was exactly what he needed.

Not only that, but he liked her. And admired her bravery. The women he dated wouldn't last an hour on the street. This girl—*woman*—was tough. But soft and sweet around the edges.

"I have a vacant flat above my garage. You can stay there as long as you need to."

She looked as if she was seriously considering it for a second, then shook her head. "No, I don't think so. I have no way to pay you."

"So you'll pay me later, when you have money."

"Suppose I never have enough money? What then? I couldn't take advantage of your hospitality. Unless…"

"Unless what?"

She shook her head. "Forget it. It's a dumb idea."

"Tell me."

"I was thinking, maybe if you needed a cook…"

He leaned forward. "You can *cook?*"

She gave him an indignant look. "I'm half Italian. Of course I can cook."

The only thing Ty enjoyed more than a beautiful woman was a home-cooked meal. Unfortunately, he hated cooking and the food his mother prepared typically had the flavor and consistency of cardboard. "What are we talking here? Just dinner, or do I get breakfast, too?"

"Do you want breakfast?"

"*Hell, yeah.* I'd say breakfast and dinner every day are definitely worth a month's rent. To be fair, I should probably give you the house and I'll take the flat."

"Oh." A shy smile curved her mouth. "The flat is fine. I don't take up much space."

"Okay, but I'm definitely getting the better end of the deal."

"And I still get to keep the cleaning job?"

"Absolutely."

"You're not going to change your mind in a month and tell me I have to sleep with you?"

That's the one thing he could offer without a hint of hesitation. "I am not going to ask you to sleep with me."

She gave him a scrutinizing look. "You promise?"

"Yes, Tina DeLuca, I *promise.*"

Four

Ty smelled fresh coffee.

He rolled over in bed, peering with one eye at the clock. It wasn't unlike his mother to pop over unannounced and cook for him, but at seven-thirty in the morning?

He stretched and scratched his chest, wincing as the tender skin smarted under the scrape of his nails, and he remembered the fiasco last night. Then he smelled something cooking, something mouthwateringly wonderful, and realized that it definitely wasn't his mother in his kitchen.

He sat up, salivary glands tingling in anticipation.

Bacon. It was definitely bacon. And despite the fact that he'd gotten less than six hours of sleep, he was out of bed and heading for the shower in a heartbeat. Within ten minutes he'd showered, shaved and dressed, and was pounding down the stairs to the kitchen.

Tina stood at the stove, poking at something in a fry-ing.pan with a wooden spoon. She saw him standing there and flashed him a bright smile. It had been close to one-thirty in the morning when he'd gotten her settled in the one bedroom flat above his garage, but she looked well-rested. Her dark hair was damp and pulled back in some sort of clip thingy, but tendrils hung loose around her face. In jeans, tennis shoes and a pink sweatshirt, she didn't look a day over seventeen. And cute. She looked damned cute.

He hadn't broken out in a cold sweat at the sight of her there and his heart rate was steady and normal.

So far so good.

"Good morning," she said. "I hope you don't mind that I let myself in. I wanted to get started on breakfast."

"Works for me," he said, taking a cup down from the cupboard and pouring himself coffee. "How's the flat? Are you comfortable?"

She breathed a blissful sigh. "It was heavenly. I haven't had a good night's sleep in days."

He stirred creamer into his cup and took a sip. Not too strong, not too weak. She brewed a hell of a pot of coffee. He was really going to like this arrangement.

"There wasn't much in the fridge so I had to improvise," she said. "I hope you like omelets."

"I'll eat pretty much anything. When you have a mother who cooks like mine, you either starve or develop an iron stomach."

Her eyebrows rose a notch. "She can't be *that* bad."

"She's worse than that bad. But she means well."

She looked as though she didn't believe him. "I made up a menu for you to approve, and I'll need some supplies."

He had figured she would just cook whatever, and he

would eat it. He had no idea he would get to choose, or that she would take this so seriously. "I'm sure anything you make will be fine and after work today we can stop at the market and pick up whatever you need."

"Have a seat, it's almost ready."

He watched from the table, practically drooling in anticipation as she rearranged the food on a plate—omelet dripping with melted cheese, strips of crispy bacon, golden fried potatoes. When she placed his plate at the kitchen table and he took his first bite, he felt like the luckiest man alive. "This is fantastic."

Her smile positively beamed with pride, and he realized just how important it was to her that she'd please him. She had no idea.

When she didn't join him at the table he asked, "You're not hungry?"

She shrugged. "I had a little something before you got up. I didn't want to impose."

"It's not an imposition. The only thing worse than my mother's cooking is eating alone. Just ask my sister. I'm always mooching meals off her and her fiancé." He gestured to the empty chair across from him. "Cop a squat, keep me company."

Almost shyly, she lowered herself into the chair, propping her feet on the edge of the seat and tucking her knees under her chin. She was close now, only a few feet away. He caught the faintest scent of soap and shampoo, and felt the slightest quickening of his pulse.

Think of her as a sister, he reminded himself.

"So, Tina DeLuca, tell me about yourself. Where are you from?"

"I grew up in Philly," she said.

"With your aunt?"

"Yeah, after my mom got sick. When she died two years later, Aunt Louise became my permanent guardian."

"How did your mom die?"

"She had ALS—Lou Gehrig's Disease."

He put his fork down. "I'm sorry."

He looked truly saddened by it. What saddened Tina the most was that so many memories of her mother had faded over the years until all that was left were vague impressions. "Aunt Louise was really good to me. That's why, when she had her stroke, I wanted to help take care of her. I was only twelve, but I started cooking and cleaning. When I was seventeen she had her second stroke and needed round-the-clock care. I dropped out of school to stay with her."

He took a sip of coffee, then picked up his fork and returned to his breakfast with gusto. He ate with the enthusiasm of a man who hadn't had a decent meal in months. To say she was flattered was a major understatement. She was just glad she could do something nice for him. He'd practically saved her life, giving her a job and a place to stay. She shuddered to think where she would be right now if not for Mae's kindness and Ty's good nature.

"Did you ever finish high school?" he asked.

"I never went back, but I got my GED, and I took some on-line college courses in my spare time. For several years the Internet was my only outlet to the outside world. My cousin Ray promised me that when Aunt Louise died, he would give me the house and half of the money. I didn't do it for the money, though. She did so much for me and my mom, I wanted to give that back to her."

"But he lied," Ty said.

She nodded. "Two weeks after she died there was a for sale sign in the window, and he was asking me to be 'nice' to him."

"Sleazy bastard," he muttered.

"I told him no way, and he told me I didn't have a choice, I *belonged* to him, and he was going to take what was rightfully his."

"Did he…?"

"He tried. But I…stopped him."

"Stopped him?"

She caught her lip between her teeth. "You're going to laugh."

"I swear, I wouldn't laugh about something like that."

"I, um, hit him over the head. With a frying pan."

The corners of Ty's mouth twitched.

"A cast-iron frying pan," she added.

He was trying really hard now not to smile.

"He was chasing me around the house, but he's really fat so I was a lot faster than him. I ran into the kitchen, grabbed the pan off the stove, and when he barged in after me, I clobbered him. The pan made a loud bong against his head and he landed so hard the whole house shook. It was kind of like something out of a Road Runner cartoon."

The amusement that had been tugging at his lips disappeared. "I guess it does sound funny when you think about it, but I'm sure it wasn't at the time. You must have been really scared."

"No, I was more disgusted than anything. I was scared *after* I hit him. At first I thought he was dead. When I realized he was still breathing, I knew he'd be really mad when he woke up. He'd call the police and they would probably take his side. I stuffed a couple of things in my bag, grabbed what money I had saved and got out of Dodge. I had a couple of leads on my father and figured it was the time to look. But the money went a lot faster than I thought it would. And here I am."

"And all your stuff is still in Philly?"

"I'm sure if I try to go back and get it, he'll have me arrested for assault."

"After sexually assaulting you, I doubt he'd be dumb enough to file charges against you." He balled his napkin and dropped it on his empty plate. "Breakfast was really good. Thanks."

He smiled at her and she went all warm and mushy inside. She wondered if he knew how gorgeous he was.

There was no way he couldn't know.

"You're half Italian," he said. "What's the other half?"

"My mom said my father was Hispanic."

"You never met him?"

"He doesn't even know about me. My mom met him while he was on leave after boot camp. They only spent a weekend together, but she said she loved him enough for a lifetime. She said he gave her the most precious gift in the world. Me."

"She told you all this?"

"No, I read it in her journal after she died. When she got sick, she started writing every day about her life, so I would never forget her. She gave it to my aunt to give to me when I turned thirteen."

"What did you say your father's name is?"

"Martin Lopez."

He stood, carrying his plate to the dishwasher. "And you say you traced him here?"

"I found *a* Martin Lopez. I just don't know if he's the *right* Martin Lopez. All I know is his name, what year he was born, that he was born in Texas, and he was in the army and finished boot camp nine months before I was born."

Ty refilled his coffee cup. "That's a lot to go on."

"You would think so, but you wouldn't believe how many men are named Martin Lopez."

"If he was in the army, can't you find him through old military records?"

"The army isn't exactly free with the information. You would have thought I was a Russian spy or something. But after two years of research, I narrowed it down to three possibilities. The first two weren't him. The third looked promising, but the address I had is an old one. Someone different lives there now and they said the Lopezes didn't leave a forwarding address, but they were pretty sure they live nearby. I looked in the phone book, but he's not listed. That's as far as I've gotten."

Ty leaned against the edge of the counter, one foot crossed over the other, looking like a blond god. His jeans were relaxed fit, his flannel shirt on the loose side, but she knew first-hand the sculpted physique all that fabric hid. She'd thought about it a lot last night after she'd settled in. She'd lain in bed, staring at the ceiling, thinking about Ty. She felt godawful for using the pepper spray on him, but she remembered the way his arms had felt wrapped around her in the shower. Solid and sure, but not intimidating. The memory of his hand cupping her breast had caused little tingles in the pit of her stomach.

But he was older and so much more sophisticated than her. To him, she was just a kid. Experience-wise, she was light years behind him.

"I'm going to make some phone calls today, see what I can find," Ty said.

She shook her head. "I don't want you calling your detective."

He dumped the last of his coffee and set his cup in the sink. "I won't need to. Real estate is my business. If your father owns a house, there has to be a deed. It shouldn't be that hard to find him."

"How long would that take?"

"A day. Two tops." He said it casually, like it was no big deal.

To her it meant everything.

In a day or two he might bring to an end a search that had spanned over two years and brought her hundreds of miles from her home. He might find the one person left in the world who could possibly care about her. Be her family.

It was official, Tyler Douglas was her hero.

It was nearly four o'clock when Ty parked his truck in front of his rental house. He walked up to the porch, a spring in his step. He was about to make Tina one very happy woman.

Girl he reminded himself. He was definitely better off thinking of her as a girl—too young and naive. And he was old enough to know better.

He unlocked the door and stepped inside, rubbing warmth into his chilled hands. "Tina!" he called, to alert her to his presence. No way he wanted another run-in with her pepper spray.

"Back here," she answered. "Cleaning the tub."

He followed her voice through the house, noting her progress. The kitchen was spotless, and when he popped his head in the fridge it no longer smelled as if he'd been storing a corpse in it. The carpet had been vacuumed, the blinds and windows polished, and when he stepped in the bathroom, the tile was so gleaming white it nearly had him reaching for his Ray-Bans.

Kneeling next to the tub was Tina, bent over, jeans snug against her swaying backside, vigorously scrubbing the drain.

A sudden tug of arousal was answered by a stab of apprehension. If he didn't get a grip he'd be breaking out in a cold sweat any minute now.

He was caught off guard, that's all. He could control this.

"Everything looks great," he said, looking anywhere but her curvy behind.

Tina looked up at him over her shoulder and smiled. "Thanks. I'm almost finished."

Her cheeks were rosy, her eyes bright. Damn, she was pretty.

She turned the faucet on and rinsed the scouring powder down the drain. Her sweatshirt sleeves were pushed up to her elbows and yellow rubber gloves covered her to her forearms. When she was finished, she stood, wiping her forehead with her sleeve. Several spirals of hair fell across her forehead and she blew them out of her eyes. "All done."

He pulled a wad of cash out of his pocket, peeled three twenties off and handed them to her. "I figured you'd prefer cash to a check."

She stripped the gloves off and dropped them in the bucket at her feet. "I thought you said minimum wage."

Yeah, that was when he was trying to get her *not* to want the job. "I said *almost* minimum wage. I paid my last cleaning woman seven dollars an hour."

"But sixty dollars would be almost seven-fifty an

hour. I don't want you paying me more than you normally would because you feel sorry for me."

"Jeez, would you just take it? You earned it." He flapped the bills in front of her until she finally took them.

"Thanks." She tucked them in the back pocket of her jeans and they walked out to the front room.

He wondered when she was going to ask him about finding her dad. She had to be curious. And he was practically bursting to tell her, because he knew it would make her happy. Considering what she'd been through lately, she deserved some happiness.

"You ready to get out of here?" he asked.

"Sure." She slipped her jacket on and slung her backpack over one shoulder. "What about that stuff," she asked, nodding to the cleaning supplies in the corner of the kitchen.

"I'll take them to the office building when the painters are finished." She followed him out the front door and he locked it behind them. "Have you got any plans for this evening?" he asked.

"I have a dinner to cook. Which means we'll have to go to the store first. I'd also like to stop by the diner and pay Mae."

He opened the truck door for her, waited until she climbed in, then walked around and got in the driver's seat. "I was thinking maybe we could eat out tonight."

She looked at him, eyebrows raised. "What would you want to do that for?"

He couldn't stand it anymore. He took the slip of paper with Martin Lopez's address out of his jacket pocket and handed it to her. "So we have time to go here."

For the longest time, she simply stared at it, her bottom lip locked tightly between her teeth. When she finally looked at him, tears glistened in her eyes. "Are you sure it's really him?"

"Yeah, and he lives less than a mile from my house. Pretty weird, huh?" When she didn't say anything else, he asked, "So, you want to go?"

She ran her fingers through her hair, looked down at her damp sweatshirt. "I'm a mess."

"So we'll stop back at the house first and you can clean up."

"I wish I had something nicer to wear. I just grabbed the bare essentials when I left. All I have is jeans."

"If I wanted to buy you a dress would you let me?"

She looked over at him and smiled. "No, but it's sweet of you to offer."

"Tina, if this guy is really your father, it isn't going to matter what you're wearing."

An hour later Tina sat in the passenger seat of Ty's truck as they drove to Martin Lopez's house, checking her reflection in the vanity mirror clipped to the visor. Sometimes she hated having naturally curly hair—most times actually. It was ungodly thick and never wanted to lie right. Any time she attempted to straighten it, she ended up with a full head of fuzz. She would never be able to accomplish the sleek, sophisticated styles that were in fashion now.

It was just so…*unruly.*

She stuck her tongue out at her reflection and snapped the visor up. "I hate my hair."

Ty glanced over at her. "You have pretty hair. You're just nervous."

She was. She was so nervous her hands were trembling and her fingers were ice-cold. She'd been nervous when she went to see the others, but not like this. Maybe because this was the last one on her list. Her last shot. It just *had* to be him. "What if he hates me? What if he doesn't want to know he has a daughter? What if I tell him who I am and he tells me to get lost?"

"That's not going to happen." He sounded so sure. She wished she could feel that confident about it.

"Here it is." He pulled up in front of a small, brick, bungalow-style house. The porch light was glowing, as if the residents had been expecting company. It was nearly dark, but Tina could tell the house was well cared for, and there were two newer-model cars parked in the driveway.

"I can't believe this is actually it."

Ty killed the headlights and shut off the engine. "Would you like me to stay in the truck?"

The thought of walking up there alone—well, her knees were so wobbly she wasn't sure she'd make it by herself. "I know it's a lot to ask considering everything you've already done for me, but could you come with me?"

He didn't look as though it was an imposition at all. He just smiled and said, "Sure."

They got out and started up the walk together and she could swear everything switched into slow motion. She stuffed her hands in her jacket pockets to keep them from shaking, and barely felt the icy wind whipping her hair into her face. Her legs were so shaky she stumbled on the steps leading up to the porch.

Ty hooked an arm through hers and hauled her close to his side. He must have felt her shaking, because he said, "Relax, it'll be fine."

He rang the bell. An eternity seemed to pass before she heard footsteps inside, and the rattle of the doorknob. She held her breath as the door finally swung open and warm light poured over her face. When she took a breath, she caught the scent of something spicy cooking inside.

"Can I help you?"

A woman peered out at them through the storm door. She was definitely Hispanic, and looked to be in her mid to late forties. She was dressed professionally, as if she had just come home from work.

Ty nudged her, but for the life of her, Tina couldn't make her mouth work. Finally he stepped forward. "Hi, my name is Tyler Douglas, and this my friend Tina DeLuca. We're looking for Martin Lopez."

"Tyler Douglas. You have that real estate office in town," she said. "Marty is my husband."

"Could we speak to him?" When she looked hesitant he added, "We won't take much of his time."

"Well, we were just sitting down to dinner..."

"Please," Tina said, suddenly feeling desperate. She'd come this far, she couldn't bear the thought of having to do this again later, or tomorrow. She wanted to know now if she'd found her father. "It's important."

Mrs. Lopez must have seen the desperation in Tina's eyes, because she unlatched the storm door and pushed it open, inviting them inside. "Marty," she called. "Someone is here to see you."

Tina and Ty stepped inside the colorfully decorated front room. The television was on and tuned to a local news station. But all that faded into the background when Martin Lopez stepped into the room, wiping his hands on a dish towel. He was older than she'd expected, maybe because she was still picturing the young man her mother had described in her journal. And there was a familiarity about him, something that clicked inside, and she realized, she was looking at a face that wasn't too dissimilar to her own. Ty must have noticed the resemblance, too, because he squeezed her arm.

"Marty, I'm going to go check on dinner," his wife said.

Martin smiled and patted her shoulder, watching her walk away, then turned back to Tina and Ty. "What can I do for you?"

Gathering every bit of courage she could muster, her heart beating so hard it was nearly bursting from her chest, Tina stepped forward and said, "Hi, I'm Tina, and I think I may be your daughter."

Five

"There must be some mistake," Martin Lopez said, looking more than a little surprised. "The only daughter I have is named Lucy."

Did that mean she had a half-sister, Tina wondered, her spirits lifting even higher. A real family? "I know it sounds crazy," she said. "But were you in the army twenty-two years ago?"

His brow furrowed in thought. "Let's see, twenty-two years ago I had just finished boot camp."

There was no way this could be coincidence. It *was* really him. "And you were in Philadelphia visiting friends?"

"Actually, yes. For about a week."

"Do you remember meeting a woman named Carmela DeLuca?"

The crease in his brow deepened and he shook his head. "The name doesn't ring a bell."

Tina pulled out a picture of her and her mother standing on the front stoop of their apartment building. Tina was only a baby and her mother cradled her close, a beaming smile on her face. "This is what she looked like."

Martin took the picture from her and studied it. "Come to think of it, she does look a little familiar. Did she work in a diner?"

"Yes!" Tina said, excitement filling her chest. She had the sudden vision of warm family gatherings and holidays spent with people who loved her. A father to give her advice and a sister to go shopping with. A family.

"I do remember her. I stopped in for a cup of coffee and we got to talking. She was just getting off work, and it was late, so I offered to walk her home."

Tina wasn't sure how to ask the next question, and settled on subtly. "She invited you inside?"

"No. I dropped her at her doorstep, then walked back to my hotel. The next day I spent with a couple of buddies from boot camp. The day after that I was on a bus home."

A sick, sinking sensation gripped her heart. "But she wrote about you in her journal. She said you spent the weekend together. She said that you fell in love with each other."

Martin shrugged. "I'm sorry. I don't know why your mother would tell you that. It's just not true. I hate to disappoint you, but there's no way I could be your father."

Ty grabbed the bag of hamburgers and the drink holder off the front seat of his truck, hopped out and shoved the door closed with his foot. Though Tina had declined his dinner invitation, he knew there was no food in her refrigerator and she was bound to get hungry.

And he was worried about her.

She'd looked so crushed when they left Martin Lopez's house and she hadn't said a word on the way home. When he'd pulled into the driveway, she'd thanked him for his help and told him she'd be over in the morning to cook his breakfast. He'd asked her if she wanted to come up to the house for a bit, but she said she wanted to be alone. The more he thought about it, the more he realized *alone* is the last thing a person should be at a time like this.

There had to be something he could do to make this easier for her. Something he could do to help.

Food in hand, he headed up the dark staircase on the side of the garage. A soft yellow glow lit the window next to the door, which meant she was probably still awake. He knocked and waited. A minute passed before he saw the curtain lift. After another brief pause, the door opened.

Backlit by the single lamp on the table next to the sofa, Tina's face was draped in shadow.

Ty held up the bag. "I know you said you weren't hungry, but I got you something anyway."

"You didn't have to do that," she said so softly he had to strain to hear her.

"Can I come in?"

After a second's hesitation, she stepped back and motioned him inside. He stepped in, and, as he set the food down on the tiny table in the kitchen nook, he noticed a dozen or so balled-up tissues on the coffee table. Either she'd been crying, or she'd developed a sudden cold. Then he saw her dab at her eyes and realized she was *still* crying. Aw, man. There had to be something he could do or say, something to make her feel better, but he was at a complete loss. He'd never felt so helpless or useless in his life.

Well, almost never.

Tina sat on the couch, tucking her knees under her chin and wrapping her arms around her legs.

He walked over to the sofa and sat next to her. "Is there anything I can do?"

She sniffed and shook her head, tears rolling down her cheeks in earnest. "I'm scared."

Her words hit Ty like a sledgehammer to his chest. He couldn't sit there and do nothing. The only thing he wanted to do, the only thing he *could* do, was hold her.

He slipped an arm around her shoulders and nudged her closer. The next thing he knew, her arms were around him and she was holding on for dear life, sobbing her heart out against his chest. Then he didn't feel quite so helpless. Maybe all she needed was to feel less alone. And just by being there with her, he was helping. Though he wasn't self-centered enough to make this about him, he couldn't help noticing that he was fine. No heart palpitations, no hyperventilating. In the span of a day, Tina had undone three months' worth of the hell he'd endured.

He felt normal again.

And even stranger, he could hold Tina this way and not have sexual feelings toward her. He'd never been this physically close to a woman without having some kind of sexual intentions. In fact, he'd never really been just friends with a woman before. Knowing he was Tina's friend felt…good. It felt really, really good.

Feeling like a whole man for the first time in months—maybe in his whole life—he rubbed Tina's back, rocked her gently until her sobs subsided.

"You probably think I'm a real basket case," she finally said, her voice muffled against his damp shirt.

He smoothed her hair back from her forehead. It was soft and curly and smelled like apples. "What I think, is that you've just had a really bad couple of weeks and needed to let it all out."

"When he walked into the room, I thought for sure it was him." Her voice was soft and full of hurt. "Why would my mother lie to me?"

"Maybe he's the one who's lying."

"What reason would he have to lie?"

He shook his head. "I don't know."

"When I was in seventh grade, we did a unit in science on genealogy. I hated it. We had to look up our family history, going back four generations, and make a family-tree poster. It was a huge project that was half our grade for the semester. And I didn't do it."

"Why not?"

"I couldn't. Aunt Louise wasn't even a blood relative. She was my mom's uncle's second wife. She didn't have any information about my mom's side of the family, and I didn't know who my father was. So I got an F."

"If you had talked to the teacher, told him the situation, he probably would have understood."

"I was too embarrassed. And it hurt too much to admit that I didn't have any family. But there was always that hope. The possibility that I might find him some day. I thrived on that hope for years. Now it's gone. There's just no hope left."

Her eyes were so full of hurt it broke Ty's heart.

"What do I do now?" she asked him. "I don't have a home or a family. I don't have resources. I don't have the education I would need to get a decent job. I have nothing."

"You do have a home. You can stay in my flat and work for me as long as you need to."

"I can't stay here forever. I can't be a cleaning lady the rest of my life."

"Then you can be a cook. You could open a restaurant."

She looked up at him and smiled, and though her eyes were red-rimmed and puffy, and her nose pink, he'd never seen her more beautiful. No woman—and he'd known quite a few—had ever looked so beautiful to him. Inside or out.

She reached up, smoothed her hand across his cheek, and the look in her eyes, the desire and longing—he knew he would never think of her as a "girl" again.

He didn't make a conscious decision to kiss her. It just sort of happened. He lowered his head, and she raised hers, and their lips were touching. And all of his good intentions, all that stuff about them just being friends, flew right out the window. He wanted her, more than he'd ever wanted a woman in maybe his whole life. But instead of losing himself in the kiss, he was suddenly all too aware of her fingers in his hair, the taste of her mouth, the scent of her skin.

He knew it was coming when he felt the first flutter of his heartbeat, but he fought it. It felt so good to kiss her, to feel like himself again. He'd thought he was cured. He'd thought this time was different.

It wasn't.

One minute he was kissing Tina as if his life depended on it, the next he was on his feet and she was sitting on the floor in front of the sofa. The panic hit with the same velocity and intensity as his desire had. It stole his breath and squeezed his chest until he was sure his heart would burst. Then he was breathing *too* fast. Desperately sucking in air, still he felt as if he were suffocating. His heart raced as adrenaline saturated his bloodstream and the edges of his vision blurred.

He knew exactly what was happening, but he was completely helpless to stop it. He wanted to curl up into a ball and ride it out, but he couldn't stop moving, couldn't stop pacing the floor like a caged animal. Sweat poured off his forehead and soaked his T-shirt but he was freezing to death. His head started to spin, and he knew that if he didn't control his breathing, if he didn't get hold of himself, he was either going to pass out or be sick. No matter how he reasoned with himself, reminded himself it was a panic attack, he couldn't think rationally. He was sure this time would be it. This time he would die.

He was so tired of this, so tired of the fear, he almost wished he would die.

"Breathe into this."

He could hear her words, but she sounded a million miles away. Then Tina shoved a paper bag up to his face and he grabbed it, holding it over his nose and mouth.

"Breathe slow and deep."

He closed his eyes and took a few deep breaths, and after a minute or two felt the dizziness begin to subside, felt the tightness in his chest ease, but the worst of it wasn't over. With all that excess adrenaline in his system, he began to shake. Deep, violent shudders that zapped every bit of strength from his arms and legs and left him feeling like a wet noodle.

Tina must have somehow realized what was going to happen. She pulled him to the couch just before his legs gave out on him, so instead of landing in a heap on the floor, he at least had a soft surface to crumple into.

Then the humiliation set in, so intense he felt sick all over again. What was she going to think of him now, now that she knew how weak he was? Christ, he was embarrassed.

He opened his eyes in time to see Tina emerge from the bedroom, her arms filled with blankets.

She stopped a few feet from him. "I need to get close enough to put these around you, okay?"

He nodded, not caring how close she got, he was so cold. He was huddled in a fetal position and no matter how hard he concentrated, he just couldn't stop shaking.

Tina draped the blankets over him and tucked them around his legs. "Is that better?"

It wasn't, but he nodded.

"I am so sorry," she said, and the look of dejection on her face made him want to throw up. She thought this was her fault. She thought she was being rejected again.

"Don't," he said through chattering teeth. "Don't apologize for something you didn't do."

"If I hadn't kissed you—"

"I kissed you, too. And it isn't your fault. It's me. I'm...defective."

She sat at the opposite end of the sofa, tucking her legs against her body. "Do you get panic attacks a lot?"

"How did you know what it was?"

"After my aunt had her first stroke she would get them. It scared the heck out of me at first. I thought she was having a heart attack. After the second and third times I started to recognize the signs. Eventually her doctor put her on a low dose of Valium and that took care of it."

"Valium won't help me."

"Maybe it would be best if I leave. If my being here upsets you—"

"I told you, it's not you. Being around any woman, *all* women, freaks me out." He rubbed the heels of his palms into his eyes. He didn't want to explain what had happened, God knows he was humiliated enough already, but if he didn't, she would go on believing it was her fault. Hell, if nothing else, his being around her had been good for him. He'd have been fine if he hadn't kissed her. "It's nothing you did. Something happened to me and I haven't been the same since."

"You mean, like a traumatic experience?"

"Yeah, it was pretty traumatic." He hugged the blankets tighter around him. He wasn't shaking as badly, and his heart rate had slowed, but he was still cold. And mortified.

"Maybe if you tell me about it you'll feel better," she said.

He hadn't told anyone, not even Matt, his best friend. But what the hell, he couldn't be any more embarrassed than he already was. She couldn't think any less of him.

He forced the words out. "I was with a woman and I couldn't…perform."

She didn't say anything. Didn't laugh and point and call him a wuss. She just watched expectantly, waiting for him to elaborate. And though he didn't know why, he kept talking.

"It had been a really bad week—I'm talking the worst—but it was finally Friday, and I just wanted to go out and get drunk and forget everything. So I did. Pretty late in the evening I ran into a girl I used to date in college. She had just been dumped by her fiancé and was in the market for revenge sex."

Tina's eyebrow quirked up.

"I know it sounds shallow. But I took her home.

Things started to get pretty hot and heavy, but I guess I'd had more to drink than I thought. No matter what she did, it just wouldn't work. I couldn't get it up."

"And how did she take this?"

"Not very well."

She didn't ask for details and he didn't offer them. It was one thing to speak in generalizations, and quite another to give her specifics, like the fact that she had laughed at him, and accused him of being gay. And those were the kindest of her words. She'd gotten downright ugly.

"I guess, looking at it from her point of view, I can understand why she was upset," Tina offered. "She gets dumped by her fiancé, and the first guy she's with rejects her, too."

"I didn't consciously reject her." He leaned back against the cushions and propped his feet on the coffee table. He felt better now, and not nearly as humiliated as he had been before. Maybe because Tina was so understanding and rational. He'd expected sympathy, but she hadn't even given him that.

"I take it, before that night, you'd never had trouble…performing?"

"No! Everything has always worked just fine. Better than fine. I've never had any complaints."

"Have you thought about talking to someone about this? Like a therapist."

"No way," he said, shaking his head. "I don't need a shrink. It's bad enough telling you. No way I'm talking to a total stranger. I'll work through this myself."

"What if you can't?"

That wasn't even an option. He'd never faced a challenge he couldn't conquer, a hurdle too high to jump.

In high school he'd broken nearly every sport record with little effort, he'd graduated college with the highest of honors and earned his first million at twenty-five. He would get over this. Granted, it was taking a bit longer than he anticipated, but once he figured out an angle, he would beat it.

"Does this only happen when you're with a woman? I mean, does everything work when you, um, fly solo?"

Fly solo? Jesus, he couldn't believe she'd just asked him that. It took an awful lot to embarrass him, but he could feel his neck heating. "Solo is the *only* way it works."

"So, physically everything's okay," she said, and he nodded. "So, all you really need to do is get over your anxiety."

He wished it were that easy. He wished he could snap his fingers and it would go away.

"What if I could help you?"

He narrowed his eyes at her. "Help me how?"

"You're comfortable around me, right? I mean, as long as we're not kissing."

Oddly enough, he was. More than he'd ever been with a woman. He felt as though he could really talk to her and she wouldn't judge him. Wouldn't think him weak.

He nodded.

"Do you trust me?"

"There are levels of trust, Tina. Are we talking, would I trust you to water my plants while I'm on vacation, or trust you with my stock portfolio?"

She grinned. "Do you believe that I would never do anything to hurt you?"

"I do," he said, surprised the words came so easily. She was so sweet, he couldn't imagine her intentionally hurting anyone for *any* reason. With the possible exception of her cousin Ray, who, as far as Ty figured, deserved a lot worse than he'd gotten.

"And you find me attractive?"

Like that wasn't already obvious. "Tina, if I didn't find you attractive, we wouldn't be sitting here discussing this."

She chewed the inside of her cheek and he swore he could see the gears in her head burning away at an idea. Then she smiled and he had the distinct impression he was in serious trouble.

"You're in luck, because I think I know exactly what we need to do."

Six

"**Y**ou want to do *what?*"

"Desensitize you."

Considering the scandalized look on Ty's face, this was going to be a tougher sell than Tina anticipated. To make this work, he would have to relinquish control, and it was pretty clear that he thrived on being in control. He was also an inherently sexual person—he would have to be for that one incident to have had such a drastic effect on him. Which probably made him desperate to fix this.

She was sure, if he would just hear her out, he would see that her idea could work.

"I'm afraid to ask what that means," Ty said.

"In essence, you'll have to unlearn everything you've learned about sex and start over."

"And how would I do that?"

"Well, we would start with the basics, like holding hands. And when holding hands no longer makes you feel anxious, we move on."

His brow furrowed. She had his attention now. "Move on to what, exactly?"

"Well, sitting close. Just being together. Kissing would probably be next." And boy, did Ty know how to kiss. Toe-curling, bone-melting, knock-your-socks-off-fantastic kisses. It had been like a slice of heaven—until he'd dumped her on the floor.

"And then?" he asked.

"Touching."

Now he looked downright intrigued. "Who gets to do the touching? You or me?"

"We both do." The thought of touching Ty, of being touched *by* Ty, made her go all warm and soft inside. If he was as skillful with his hands as he was with his mouth, things could get very interesting.

He cleared his throat. "And, um, where exactly will we be touching each other?"

She shrugged and tried to keep her voice casual. "Eventually, *everywhere.*" She noted the hint of panic in his eyes, and quickly added, "But that would be *way* down the road. We would take it very slow."

She saw his Adam's apple bob as he swallowed. "And when we've touched everywhere there is to touch, what then? How far are you planning to take this?"

How far indeed? It wasn't as though she'd been saving herself for marriage, or even for true love. Her circumstances had kept her virginity intact. She was in no rush to give it up, nor was she desperate to hang on to it. She figured, when the time was right, when she was ready, she would know. "Why don't we just take it a step at a time and see what happens," she offered, and that seemed to sound good to him, too, because he nodded.

He was silent for a minute, then he asked, "Why would you do this for me? Why help me?"

"That's the way it works. You help me, I help you." She thought of her cousin Ray and added, "At least, that's how it's supposed to work."

He dropped his head back and rubbed his eyes with the heels of his palms again. He let the blanket fall away, so she guessed his body temperature was back up, and as far as she could tell his breathing and heart rate were back to normal, too. He'd lost that ghastly white cast and scarlet smudges rode high across the arch of each cheek. She'd talked him through it, which meant he did trust her. But would he accept her help?

It's not like she had anything else to do—any direction in her life. It would give her time to weigh her options, to decide what she wanted to do. Since finding her father had turned into an impossibility, maybe it was time to accept that she was on her own.

"So, what do you think?" she asked.

He sat up, propping his elbows on his knees and resting his chin on his fisted hands. "In a weird way, what you're saying makes a lot of sense. But I don't know…"

"Ty, give me your hand."

He looked over at her, a flash of apprehension in his eyes.

She held out her own hand, letting it rest between them on the cushion. "No pressure: No expectations. Just a simple touch."

He reached out and laid his hand over hers. She didn't say a word, or move a muscle. She just let him get used to the feel of it. He was tense at first, but after a few minutes he relaxed. He even stroked the side of her palm with his thumb.

"See," she said, "all we have to do is to take the pressure off. Take it slow."

He still didn't look completely convinced. "You're sure you want to do this? It's been months now and it's only gotten worse. There's no telling how long it'll take me to get back to normal."

"To be honest, the farthest I've ever gone with a guy is to make out in the back seat of a car. So slow works for me, too."

He gave her an honest-to-goodness grin and a genuine look of disbelief. "A twenty-one-year-old virgin, huh? You don't see too many of those."

"It was purely by circumstance, believe me."

"You know, if this wasn't happening to me, virgin or not, I would have been trying like hell to get you into bed."

And he would have succeeded. Maybe not right away, but eventually. A girl could take only so many mesmerizing looks from his ocean-blue eyes, she could only endure so many of his bone-melting kisses and tender touches before good sense and propriety gave way to need and desire.

A week tops and she would have been putty in his hands.

"I'm glad I didn't," he said, gliding his thumb up and down the center of her palm. Back and forth, so light it was barely a caress. If she didn't know better, she would think he was trying to seduce her right now. And she felt every pass deep in the center of her body—a sweet tug of longing that was completely foreign to her. He charmed her without the slightest bit of effort.

"I really like you, Tina." He idly traced the lines on

her palm. "I'm glad we were able to become friends before all the sex stuff got in the way."

Goodness, he was smooth! She could almost feel
herself swooning. He knew exactly what buttons to
push, and his delivery was so sincere, she couldn't *not*
believe him. "If that's a line, it's a damned good one."

He gave her hand a squeeze. "I think we're past lines,
don't you?"

It took a second for his meaning to sink in. "Does that
mean we're on?"

He shook his head and laughed lightly. "I keep trying to come up with a good reason to say no, and so far
I haven't found one. The truth is, I'm sick of this, of feeling like half a man. I want to fix it, no matter what it
takes." He looked up at her and grinned. "So, yeah, I
guess that means we're on."

"God, that smells good." Ty hovered behind Tina,
looking over her shoulder into the pot of spaghetti sauce
that had been simmering since before they left for work
that morning. Had it not been for their conversation last
night, he probably would have avoided being in such
close proximity—so close he could smell the flowery
scent of her soap, the faintest hint of baby powder on
her skin. But he was okay. No racing heart, no labored
breathing, no dizziness.

The fear that had gripped him only days before had
transformed into hope. He could do this. He could beat
this fear and be normal again.

Last night, they'd sat on the couch in her flat eating
cold hamburgers and fries and talking until almost midnight. When he'd finally left, she'd walked him to the
door. She'd smiled and taken his hand, and held it for a

minute. He had known it was her way of saying that was as far as it would go. She hadn't expected a kiss good-night, or even an embrace. Just a simple touch.

He'd felt a little as though he'd been zapped back in time to the fourth grade when he'd held hands with a girl for the first time on the school playground. Of course, back then he still thought it was kinda gross. Girls in general confused the hell out of him at that age. Come to think of it, they still did in a lot of ways. Except Tina. She didn't play games, or put up fronts. She didn't have ulterior motives. She was probably the most honest, genuinely nice woman he'd ever known.

And a damned good cook.

He reached around her for the spoon, and she smacked his hand away. "Ouch! Come on, can't I just have a little taste?"

"You'll spoil your appetite." Tina shooed him away. "Go do something, would you? I'm tired of you breathing down my neck."

"I can't help it. This is a novelty for me. My mom can't cook, and my sister Emily tries really hard, but she doesn't have a domestic bone in her body."

She dropped a pinch of salt in a pot of boiling water, then emptied a box of angel hair pasta in, stirring until it was all submerged. "What about you? You can't cook either?"

"It's a family thing, I guess." The sweet, spicy aroma drew him closer to the pot, closer to Tina. He was having a tough time deciding which smelled better, her or the sauce. Which would be more edible? Feeling brave, he laid his hand on the shoulder of her pink sweatshirt. She glanced back at him and smiled, but didn't say anything. Her curls were piled haphazardly on the back of her head and held in place by some sort of funky-looking clip, leaving exposed the curve where her neck met her shoulder. He couldn't wait to press kisses there, to taste her olive-tinted skin. He was betting, as amazing as that sauce probably tasted, Tina would taste a million times better.

He moved his thumb a fraction, until he hit bare skin—felt her shiver—and his heart gave an answering jolt in his chest. Too much too soon, he realized, pulling his hand away. Too intimate, too…something that he obviously wasn't ready for. But rather than let himself feel discouraged, he was just thankful he could stand as close as he was. He *could* touch her, even if that meant only holding her hand. He could sit in a quiet room with her and just talk—about work, or movies, or whatever—and not wonder all the while how he would persuade her into bed.

The buzzer on the stove sounded and she opened the oven door. The mouthwatering aroma of toasted butter and garlic escaped on a rush of hot air, tempting his taste buds. She bent over to peer inside, her jeans pulling snug against her behind. Though she was tiny—nearly a foot shorter than his own six-one—she packed some voluptuous curves into that petite frame, although it was difficult to distinguish them under the oversized sweatshirts she always wore. Then he got to thinking, as far as clothes went, she probably didn't have much of a selection. Most of her things were still at her aunt's house.

Maybe it was time to do something about that.

"It's only going to be another minute or two before everything is ready," Tina said. "Why don't you set the table."

Ty opened the cupboard above his head and pulled

two plates down. "I was thinking, I have a business trip to take this weekend and I wondered if you might like to come along with me. We would drive out Saturday morning, spend one night, then come back Sunday."

"What kind of business trip?"

"A, um, property dispute. I have a few loose ends to tie up." And one disgusting pig to take care of. He really hoped Cousin Ray gave them a hard time, so Ty would have a good reason to teach him a lesson. He didn't typically condone violence, but in this case, the punishment fit the crime. "It's about an eight-hour drive, so I would enjoy the company."

She pulled the tray of garlic bread from the oven and set it on the stove. "Sure, I'll go."

"Great." Ty set the plates and utensils on the table as Tina carried the food over. He sat down and was reaching for a slice of bread, his mouth watering in anticipation, when the doorbell rang. "Oh, man, who is that?"

He looked so devastated by the interruption, Tina had to smile. "I'll fix our plates while you see who it is," she said.

He was grumbling to himself as he pushed back his chair and headed to the front door. Tina fixed Ty's plate with a healthy serving of pasta, steamed green beans, and bread, then served herself.

She ladled sauce over the pasta and topped it with fresh parmesan cheese. This morning she'd scrounged up the ingredients she'd needed to get the sauce started, and after work she and Ty had gone to the grocery store. And boy, had she gotten weird looks as they'd strolled up and down the aisles together. But Ty had been a perfect gentlemen, introducing her as his friend. It was a lot less demeaning than referring to her as his cleaning lady, or his cook. Not that she was ashamed of making an honest living. She just didn't want people to get the wrong idea about their relationship.

She may have been young and inexperienced but she wasn't naive. She could see that Ty was a well-liked, successful member of the community—and way out of her class. The sprawling Cape Cod he lived in, though old, was completely renovated and the interior, though a tad impersonal in her opinion, carried the mark of a decorator. The lawn was well tended and looked professionally landscaped.

Ty obviously made a good living and this was a small town. What would people think of him hanging out with the hired help? And what would they think of her?

Tina heard voices, and turned to see Ty standing in the kitchen doorway, an older woman beside him. She was a shorter, thinner version of her Ty. Same pale-blond hair and sea-blue eyes. Any similarities stopped right there. Where Ty was about as easygoing as a man could be, his mother stood stiff and staunch in her designer suit. Her hair was teased and whipped into an indestructible shell not even a hurricane could dislodge and a thick veneer of flawlessly applied makeup gave her a plastic, almost lifeless appearance. Her eyes had that stretched look of someone who'd taken one too many trips to the plastic surgeon.

Hoity toity—that's what Tina's aunt would have called her.

She gave Tina a thorough once-over, a delicate little crinkle forming in her brow. Then the crinkle deepened to a look of downright contempt. A look Tina was all too familiar with.

Mae's diner. Ty's mother had been sitting at the table next to Tina's. She'd given Tina a dirty look—the identical look she was giving her now—when Tina had told Mae she couldn't pay her bill.

What were the odds?

"See, here she is," Ty said to his mother. "Tina, this is my mom. Mom, this is Tina."

Oh, boy, this was going to be tough to explain. And she could see that an explanation was exactly what Mrs. Douglas expected. Of all the people in the world to witness the most embarrassing, humiliating experience in her life, it just had to be Ty's mother. The powers that be had a really warped sense of humor.

"I guess you're surprised to see me here," Tina said.

"Indeed I am," Mrs. Douglas said, not bothering to mask the contempt in her voice.

Ty looked back and forth between the two of them. "Do you know each other?"

"Sort of. She was sitting by me in the diner the other day," Tina explained. "When I couldn't pay."

"She's a con artist," his mother said. "And why you have her in your home, I can't even imagine."

Oh, this was bad.

Ty laid a hand on his mother's shoulder, his voice calm and reasonable. "I told you, she's my cook, and what happened at Mae's was just a misunderstanding. We went over there this afternoon and Tina paid her back."

Mrs. Douglas didn't look the least bit pacified by his explanation. "She paid her, or *you* paid her?"

"Tina did," he said, sounding completely unaffected by her disapproving tone. Maybe he was used to it.

"I don't understand why you would pay for a cook," she said, with a huffy quality that made it clear Tina's cooking for her son was some sort of personal slight. "You can always eat with your father and me."

"I'm not paying her. She cooks in exchange for rent."

Her eyes widened and she let out a gasp. "She *lives* here? She's just a child. What will people think?"

Though she wouldn't have guessed it possible, Tina was liking this woman less and less.

Ty shrugged it off. "You worry too much about what other people think, Mom." He slipped an arm around her shoulder. "We were just sitting down to eat, so I'll walk you to the door."

Mrs. Douglas flashed Tina one final scathing look before she let her son lead her out of the room. Tina collapsed into her chair, knowing she hadn't done a thing to deserve the woman's antipathy, but feeling guilty anyway. A few minutes later, Ty returned, looking none the worse for wear.

"Sorry about that," he said, taking a seat across from her. "My mom can be a piece of work sometimes."

"She really doesn't like me."

Ty shrugged. "She'll get over it. Now, let's eat."

His breezy attitude did little to ease her guilt—though what she was feeling guilty for, she wasn't exactly sure. She wished she could brush off his mother's harsh treatment as easily as he could. It wasn't just that Ty's mother didn't like her, she had made Tina feel…cheap. As if she had something to be ashamed about.

Tina wasn't ashamed of her past, she also didn't need reminding that she wasn't good enough for someone like Ty. They were from different worlds, and eventually that would catch up to them.

Across the table Ty forked a mouthful of spaghetti and moaned with pleasure. "This is the most amazing thing I've ever tasted." He gestured to her plate. "Aren't you going to eat?"

Tina looked down at her plate and realized she'd completely lost her appetite.

Seven

Ty wasn't typically the kind of guy to force a woman into doing something against her will. In fact he could usually charm a woman into doing pretty much whatever he wanted. But he knew if he told Tina where they were going, no amount of charm in the world would have gotten her into his truck that morning. Which is why he hadn't told her. Why he instead had tried to keep her distracted, talking about anything but their intended destination.

Fall had erupted almost overnight, and a kaleidoscope of reds and oranges and vibrant yellows passed in a blur as they reached the southeastern edge of the state. They had been on the road for over an hour when Tina asked where it was exactly that they were headed to—too long to turn back. Not that she didn't ask him to do just that.

Demanded it, in fact.

"I don't want to go back to Philadelphia," she said, her hand tensing in his. They'd been holding hands most of the trip. In fact, they held hands the majority of the time they were together now. He could tell himself it was all part of the process, when the truth was, he just liked being close to her. Liked touching her.

Probably liked it too much, and for some reason he didn't understand, that didn't scare the hell out of him. He didn't do the whole emotional attachment thing. Didn't let himself get that close to a woman.

He felt close to Tina.

"You said this was a business trip," Tina said, genuine fear leaking into her tone. But she didn't have to worry, he would protect her.

"It is. The business of getting your stuff back."

"What if he has me arrested?"

"He won't." He squeezed her hand. "Tina, I'm not going to let him hurt you. I'm not going to let *anyone* hurt you."

She didn't look as though she believed him.

He tugged on her hand. "Come here. Sit next to me."

She unbuckled her seatbelt, slid across the bench and rebuckled herself into the center seat. He put an arm around her and she leaned into him. They'd sat this way last night on the couch in his living room while they'd watched a rental movie. At first he'd been driven to distraction by the softness of her hair brushing against his chin, the warmth of her body pressed alongside him. She always smelled so damned good. Sweet, like baby powder, with a tinge of something exotic lurking underneath. He'd spent the first quarter of the movie hyperaware of every move she made, every nuance—the rise and fall of her breasts as she breathed, the moist heat of her breath where she let her head rest on his shoulder.

Though rationally he knew it wouldn't go any farther than a cuddle, it had taken his body a while to catch onto the concept. At first his heart had pounded relentlessly and sweat had beaded his brow. It had both amazed and frustrated the hell out of him that something as simple as sitting close to Tina could screw with his head so damned badly. But gradually he'd begun to relax. He stopped thinking about what might happen and let the simplicity of their situation sink in. Then he was okay. Better than okay, really.

He realized later, after he'd walked her to her door, it was the first time since high school that he'd sat down to watch a video with a woman and actually made it to the end of the movie. Not that he didn't like watching movies, but sex usually got in the way.

That he was able to just spend time with a woman made him feel surprisingly good. Proud almost.

"What if he threw my stuff out?" Tina asked. "What if it's all gone?"

"Then he's going to replace it all." Ty didn't add the "or else" that was sitting on the tip of his tongue. He would see to it that Ray the sleazebag would make good by Tina.

"It feels so weird to be going back. When I left, I thought it was for good."

"You don't miss it?"

She shrugged. "It's just a place. From the time I was seventeen, I didn't have much of a life. My life, my friends, were all on the Internet. They're the only people I miss. That was my only link to the outside world. But when I left, I couldn't exactly drag my computer along."

"You should have told me. I have a computer at home you could have used."

"It's okay. I haven't really had the opportunity. We've been spending so much time together."

"Too much time?" he asked, the possibility sparking an odd sense of disappointment. Had he been enjoying their time together more than she had?

She smiled up at him. "No, of course not. Given the choice, I'll pick a live person over a chat room or e-mail any day. I like spending time with you. It's…comfortable."

"Not exciting or passionate," he teased. "Just *comfortable.*"

No, Tina thought, the passionate part was definitely there, simmering below the surface. When they set it loose, she knew it would knock her off her feet. The mere thought of what Ty would someday soon be capable of left her excited and intrigued all at once. The only thing that kept her hinged was knowing they were going to take it slow. Otherwise, she might not have been able to handle a man like him.

"Comfortable is nice," she told him. "I've never been the type to want excitement. I've learned to appreciate the simple things in life. And I know this would make most men run screaming in the opposite direction, but I would probably be happiest as a wife and mother. There's no career I desire, no job I can think of that would be more fulfilling than raising a family. I've always wanted a family." When he didn't say anything, she glanced up at him and said, "See, I've completely freaked you out, haven't I?"

"No. I think it's important for kids to have a mother around. Besides charity stuff, my mom never worked outside of the house. But you're right, when a woman

I'm dating starts to go domestic on me, I usually can't get away fast enough. But only because I'm not ready to settle down. Someday I'd like a family. I always figured, when the time was right, I would know."

And Tina didn't doubt that he would make some lucky woman one heck of a wonderful husband. He was considerate, kind, affectionate. And honest. He might have been a womanizer before, at least, that was the way he painted it, but she was sure that when he chose a woman to spend the rest of his life with, he would be faithful. It was sad really that they weren't better suited, because she could imagine falling in love with Ty. She might even love him a little already.

She sighed and rested her head on his shoulder, smelled his aftershave mixed with the subtle scent of leather—clean and masculine and just a touch musky. Heat from the vents in the dash warmed her cheeks and lifted her hair back from her face. It jogged loose a memory of riding in the car with her mother. It had been winter and the vinyl seat was so cold it bit through the fabric of Tina's pants and made her teeth chatter. The vision was vague and fogged with age, but she distinctly remembered leaning forward, as far as the seatbelt would allow, and pressing her hands to the heat vent. The hot air seeped through the thick knit material of her pink mittens, making her fingers feel toasty warm. Beside her, her mother smiled and hummed while she drove. She was always smiling and humming and singing to herself. Even after she was ill, she always had a smile for Tina.

Even though Tina knew she was sick—her mother was always honest with her, even about bad things—it hadn't really sunk in. At first she didn't look sick, or act sick. To her childish mind the stretch between her mother's diagnosis and her death had seemed like an eternity. But the day had finally come when Mommy could no longer run and play with her in the backyard. She would sit on the back stoop, smiling and clapping her hands as Tina rolled and tumbled through the grass.

After a while, her mother couldn't come outside anymore. She would lie on the couch watching television, or listening to the radio. She couldn't tuck Tina in to bed at night anymore either, or sing her songs. Aunt Louise tried, but she didn't know any of the special songs her mother sang, and didn't have the same sweet, angelic voice. She sounded more like a frog. And when she read Tina bedtime stories, she didn't change her voice for the different characters.

Finally the day came that her mother stopped getting out of bed. She lay quietly, looking small and ashen, her skin so translucent and fragile-looking Tina had been afraid to touch her, afraid she would break. A nurse started coming to the house every day. There were machines around the bed and wires and tubes crisscrossing every which way. And when her mother opened her eyes to look at Tina, it was as if she didn't really see her. Then she stopped opening her eyes when Tina called her name.

"It won't be long now," her aunt had begun to say, and Tina knew what that meant. Mommy was going to go to heaven to be with grandma and grandpa.

Tina didn't remember much about the day she died, or even the funeral. Only that the dress she'd worn had lace that made her itch and the shiny black shoes her aunt bought her pinched her toes. She didn't remember feeling particularly sad, but was sure she had been. She also knew Mommy had been very sick, and in heaven people didn't get sick or hurt. They floated around in the clouds, silvery wings flowing, feeling happy and peaceful. Sometimes Tina would lie in the grass and look up at the sky and try to see her. Maybe the concept of death had been too complex for her to grasp at such a young age. She didn't really begin to miss her mother until later, when at seventeen she was left with the burden of caring for her aunt.

And times like now, when she had no one else in the world. People with families didn't know how lucky they were.

"You're so quiet," Ty said. "What are you thinking about?"

"Family. Are you close with yours?"

"Emily and I are twins, so you can't get much closer than that, and I don't usually go for more than a few days without seeing my parents. They can be a little overbearing at times, but they're basically good people. They were always a little harder on Em than me."

"Why is that?"

"She didn't fit the mold. My mom wanted a little girl she could dress in frilly outfits and have tea parties with. Em is a tomboy through and through. The harder my mom pushed to change her, the harder Em pushed back. They've always been at odds."

"Your mom never tried to change you?"

"She never needed to. I always did what was expected of me. I got straight A's in school, lettered in sports. I never got in trouble. I was a good kid."

"Sounds like you worked hard to win their approval."

"That's the weird thing," he said, absently twirling a lock of her hair around his finger as he spoke. "I *didn't* work hard. I never had to. Everything just sort of came naturally for me."

Why did that not surprise her? He oozed perfection from every pore. Of course, perfect people were never really one-hundred-percent perfect. Everyone had a flaw. Ironically, his infallible confidence was probably his worst enemy right now. "You're a Golden Child."

"Sort of, I guess, although admitting it makes me feel like a snob."

"Believe me, Ty, you are not a snob. But it does explain a lot."

"Like what?"

"Like why you have no coping skills. Why what happened to you was so devastating."

When he didn't say anything, she looked up and saw that his brow had dipped low and tiny creases marked the corners of his eyes. He looked—*hurt*. She'd wounded his pride.

Ty had a softer, vulnerable side. Go figure.

"Ty, have you ever had to work for anything in your life?"

"I work damned hard," he said indignantly.

"I know that, what I mean is, have you ever had a major problem to solve that you couldn't fix? Before the thing with that woman, have you ever felt like a failure?"

He gave it some thought, then said, "No, not really."

"You never failed an important test in school? Had an important business deal go south? Have you ever done anything that made your parents really disappointed in you?"

He shrugged. "Little stuff, I guess, but nothing major."

"Ever have someone close to you die?"

"My grandma died when I was three, but I don't really remember her."

"So before that night, you'd never had anything really bad happen to you?"

The furrow in his brow deepened and he shifted uncomfortably in his seat. "Now that I think about it, I guess I haven't."

"So when something finally did happen, you had no idea how to process it, how to cope. What most people learn when they're a child, you never grasped. You were never given the chance to learn it because your life was storybook perfect."

That defensive tone crept back into his voice. "Having a good life should be a good thing, Tina."

"Yes, but sometimes bad things happening make you appreciate the good even more."

Damned if she wasn't right about that. He'd never really appreciated his perfect life, hadn't even realized he'd had one, until it was snatched away from him. It's as if he'd been walking around with his head in the clouds his entire life. He felt…abnormal.

He swore softly under his breath. "So what you're saying is, by having a good life, I'm screwed?"

"Of course not. You just have to learn to cope with failure."

"So, I'm weak?"

"It has nothing to do with strength or weakness. You have to learn what you didn't learn as a kid."

"You make it sound so simple."

"I wouldn't say simple, but not impossible either."

The more he thought about it, the more he realized she was right. Rather than cope with what had happened, his solution to the problem had been to ignore it. And when ignoring it hadn't worked, he'd been at a loss.

Where would he be right now if he hadn't met Tina? If he'd turned her away without a job? He shuddered to think what his life would be like without her in it.

But she was in it now, and that was all that mattered.

Eight

"It doesn't look like anyone is home," Ty said as he pulled into an empty spot on the narrow, tree-lined street in front of the well-kept, historical row house. Though Ty didn't keep up on the real estate market in Philly, he was guessing, considering the affluent area, the house Tina had lived in could catch a handsome price. Handsome, as in, the quarter-million range at least—probably more. He wondered if Tina had the slightest clue just how thoroughly she'd been screwed.

"I'm nervous," Tina said, peering up at the shuttered windows. "What if he shows up while we're here?"

I hope he does, Ty thought. "We'll deal with it then. Now, let's go get your stuff."

They both got out and walked together up the cobblestone sidewalk to the front door. Leaves skittered around their feet, chased down the street by the chilly wind. Hair blowing wildly around her face, Tina pulled a key ring from the front pocket on her backpack, selected a key, and slipped it in the lock.

"Uh-oh." She wiggled the key, but it wouldn't turn. "This is the key. It should work."

"He changed the locks." Ty's fists clenched. One more crime to add to a growing list. Slimy son-of-a—

"I should have known he would do this," Tina said, her voice quivering with anger. "As if he hasn't done enough already."

"Does this place have a back door?"

"You don't think he would have changed that one, too?"

"I'm sure he did. But a helluva lot less people are going to see me busting down the door in the back."

"Let's just go, Ty. I'll get new clothes. It's not worth getting arrested."

"We're not going to get arrested. Do you have a valid driver's license with this address listed as your residence?"

She nodded.

"Then you live here, and you have every right to go in and take what belongs to you."

"There's an alley around back. We'll have to walk down to the end of the street."

He grabbed her hand, lacing his fingers through hers. "Let's go."

"Well, this is convenient." Tina opened another box from the stack on the living room floor marked Goodwill. Like the others, it was filled with her belongings. Her clothes mostly. Her computer was nowhere in the house and she'd found the contents of her desk in a trash can next to the garage—pages and pages of information she'd gathered when she was searching for her father. All useless, and all in vain.

The house itself looked barren. Pictures no longer hung on the walls and the majority of the furniture was gone. The kitchen cupboards had been emptied and what remained was boxed for Goodwill.

"Ray didn't waste any time clearing out his mother's belongings, did he?" Tina shook her head, feeling inexplicably sad. This had been her home for most of her life. Now Aunt Louise was gone and she'd lost all hope of finding her father. The thought filled her with a sadness so deep, so biting, it hurt to breathe.

For the first time since her mother had died, she truly felt like an orphan.

"Come here." Ty eased her into his arms and cradled her gently against him, stroking his fingers through her hair. Somehow he always knew just what to do.

She closed her eyes and pressed her cheek to the soft flannel of his shirt. Knowing how much Ty cared washed away some of the loneliness, and at the same time it had her longing for something she knew she could never have. He would never know how much his being here meant to her, but she knew that if she tried to tell him, she would dissolve into a blubbering mess. Instead she wrapped her arms around his waist under his leather jacket and hugged him close, drawing on his strength. His body felt solid and stable and sure.

She felt protected. Loved even, if only in a friendly way.

"I want to fix this for you. I want to make it all better, make *you* better, but I know I can't." Ty kissed the top of her head. "I'm not used to this. Feeling so…helpless."

She knew she shouldn't, that he might not be ready,

but she couldn't stop herself. She rose up on her tiptoes and pressed a kiss to his cheek. The skin was warm and soft with just a hint of stubble, and she had to force herself not to linger too long, to give him the space she knew he needed. She'd never imagined herself playing the role of the aggressor, especially with a man like Ty, but she found herself eager for him to take the next step, to kiss her again.

He gazed down at her, his face absent of the apprehension she suspected he would be experiencing. "That was nice."

She smiled up at him. "Yes, it was."

He blew her away by asking, "Can you do it again?"

Her heart skipped in her chest. "Are you sure you're ready for that?"

He cupped her cheek in his palm and her legs went squishy on her. "I guess we're about to find out."

She rose up on wobbly legs, pressing her lips to his cheek. This time a fraction closer to his mouth and she let it linger a few seconds longer. Ty sighed and closed his eyes. His fingers slipped across her cheek and into her hair.

When she pulled away, his eyes were still closed. Thinking she might have gone too far that time, she felt a flash of guilt, then Ty said, "Again."

Her heart began to throb a relentless, dizzying beat. Ty slipped his fingers deeper through her hair and cupped the back of her head. As she rose up, he guided her head so that the kiss landed at the very corner of his mouth. She could feel his warm breath on her cheek, the hint of stubble where her chin brushed his. He smelled like fresh air and coffee and something inherently sexy. An essence no cologne could hope to capture.

She flattened her hands against the front of his shirt over his chest. Through the thick flannel she could feel the heavy thud of his pulse, and wondered if she'd gone too far. Still, she lingered there several seconds, until the draw of his lips, the heat of his mouth, was almost too much to resist and she backed off again.

"That felt so nice," he whispered, his fingers tangling in the back of her hair, easing her head up so he could see her face. His eyes were heavy-lidded and dark with desire. "Let's do that again."

This time he lowered his head, met her halfway, and though she was aiming for his cheek, he shifted at the last second and her lips touched his. A fierce jolt of excitement and lust swept through her, draining the last bit of strength from her already wobbly legs, yet somehow she managed to stay on her feet.

His mouth brushed lightly across hers—once, twice—then he cupped the back of her head, drawing her even closer. She felt the full weight of his lips, a trace of dampness as they parted slightly. Every female nerve ending she possessed ignited and shouted, yes! Her fingers curled into the fabric of his shirt. Her breath came faster and her heart swelled to fill her chest.

More, her body chanted. Give me more. But she knew better than to push. No matter how badly she wanted it, she knew she had to let him set the pace. Too far too fast would only set him back. He was trusting her to be the responsible one, the one to keep her head.

The tightening of his hand on the back of her head and the increase of his heart rate were both subtle clues that this was getting out of hand. She had to put on the brakes. Drawing the will to resist from what sliver of rationality she had left, she let her lips linger on his for another few seconds then slowly pulled away. But when she tried to back out of his arms, to give him space, he held her firmly against him, tucking her head under his chin. She could feel his pulse throb against her cheek, feel his unsteady breathing.

"Ty—"

"I'm okay," he said, sounding a little breathless. "It was just enough."

Funny, but she didn't know if "just enough" fit anywhere in the dynamics of their relationship. Not for her anyway. They'd barely begun, and already she was looking ahead to the next step—to ten next steps. Given her lack of experience she should at least be a little nervous about what could happen. Instead she felt…wanton.

"I've never kissed a woman like that before," Ty said. "It was…I don't know…reverent? Does that sound stupid?"

"It doesn't sound stupid at all." Although for her the kiss had been more erotic than anything. Another indicator that she was way out of her league with a man like Ty.

"I can't even remember the last time I kissed a woman and didn't have my tongue in her mouth. Come to think of it, I don't know if I ever have."

Why did that not surprise her in the least? What rational woman wouldn't want Ty's tongue in her mouth? She did.

He absently twirled a lock of her hair around his finger. "This is nice. That we can talk like this, I mean. I've never talked with a woman the way I do with you."

She wondered what that meant. Was it his way of saying he thought of her as more of a friend, or that it gave their relationship some deeper meaning? Or was she over-thinking it? "I like this, too," she said.

"But I suppose we should get this stuff out to the truck then find a place to stay for the night." He let his arms fall from around her.

Give him space. Don't push.

"We probably should," she agreed, backing away. She would feel a whole lot better when they were packed up and out of here for good. Then she could officially put this behind her and start fresh.

"Do you want to take it all?" he asked.

"Just my clothes and the box of photos sitting outside by the trash."

"You're sure?"

"There's nothing else here I want to keep." And until she found a permanent home, a permanent life, she didn't want to burden herself with too many belongings to haul around. "I'm going to check the rest of the house to make sure there aren't any more pictures. I don't want to leave those behind."

"I'll get started carrying these boxes out."

Ty watched Tina climb the stairs to the second floor, letting his eyes wander up the length of her shapely legs, the full curve of her backside, until she'd disappeared from sight.

He'd gone hard the instant she'd kissed his cheek. Usually that was all it took to start the panic, but this time had been different. Probably because he knew she wouldn't push him. He trusted her. That's also why he knew a peck on the cheek wasn't enough. He wanted to feel her lips again. He was ready for that next step. It had felt so damned good to kiss her again. She'd tasted so sweet and smelled fantastic. It was also a good thing she'd pulled away when she had. He'd been half a second away from deepening the kiss, and he wasn't sure what that would have done to him.

Maybe nothing. Maybe he'd try it again later that night and find out.

He hefted several boxes onto one arm and shouldered his way out the front door. Four trips later he'd packed all the clothes and the box of photos from out back into the bed of the truck. He walked to the bottom of the stairs and called up to Tina, "You almost ready?"

"Be right there!" She appeared on the landing a moment later, another small box in her arms. As she started down toward him, her full breasts bounced beneath her sweatshirt. He would never say it to her face for fear that he would sound like a letch, but he really couldn't wait to touch them. He was, by nature, a breast man through and through. He'd even dreamed about hers. He'd dreamed about cupping their weight in his hands, of teasing them with his tongue. He knew from the incident in the shower that they were full and supple with dark crests.

"I found a few more pictures," Tina said, handing him the box.

He held it in front of him, to hide the sudden conspicuous lack of space in the front of his jeans. It felt great to have a hard-on around a woman again, even if he couldn't use it. With each new day, each day with Tina, he began to feel more and more like his old self.

"That's all of it," Tina said. "We can get out of here now."

"Great, I'm ready for some chow." And possibly a cold shower.

They walked side by side to the front door. "Do you think we should call Ray and warn him about the broken glass in the back door? I'd hate to be responsible for the house being broken into. Not that there's much left to steal."

Ty pulled the door open for Tina, a grin spreading across his face when he looked outside. "Looks like we won't have to."

Nine

"Oh, swell," Tina muttered under her breath, confirming that the short, fat, dumpy man with beady eyes barreling up the sidewalk toward them was indeed Cousin Ray. This day just kept getting better. And as he got closer, Ty saw something that made his smile even wider—a big red lump right in the middle of Ray's receding hairline.

Way to go, Tina.

"Put it all back or I swear to God I'll call the cops," Ray said, waving a cell phone. "You have no right going into *my* house, stealing *my* things."

Tina sank back, stumbled on the step and collided with Ty's chest. He grabbed her upper arms to steady her and could feel the tension in her muscles.

She was genuinely intimidated. And who wouldn't be after being sexually assaulted by the guy?

Ty, on the other hand, wasn't intimidated. He'd been looking forward to this.

He eased himself between Tina and the slimy worm, and the slimy worm must not have known he was there, because when he saw Ty, he stopped dead in his tracks.

He was the worst kind of sleazy loser. The kind who had so many shortcomings, was such a weasely jerk, he got off on tearing other people down. People like Tina.

Not today. Today *he* was the one coming down a peg or two.

"Tina came to collect her things," Ty said. No room for argument. Just the facts. "And you're not going to stand in her way."

Ray took a full step back. "What'd you do, Tina? Bring a bodyguard?"

"Yeah," Ty said. "And I'm in the mood to rip someone apart."

Tina grabbed his arm and stepped from behind him. "No one is ripping anyone apart."

"You assaulted me!" Ray thrust a stubby finger at her. "I should call the cops and report you."

Which meant he probably hadn't yet reported her to the police, as Ty had originally suspected. And he wouldn't now either. He didn't have the balls. He was all about empty threats and accusations.

Scum.

"You do that, Ray," Tina said, her voice strong and confident. "And while you're waiting for them to show up, I'll be down at the police station filing a sexual assault report against you."

"You can't prove nothing," Ray said, but his voice lost its cocky edge. "I got marks on me. You coulda *killed* me!"

"I guess I'll just have to try harder next time." She took a step forward, and Ray actually took a nervous step back, making it pretty clear who had the upper hand now.

"Look, I didn't come here looking for trouble, Ray. I came to get my clothes, that's it. You want to drag the police into this, fine. Call them. But who do you think they're going to believe? Is that even a chance you're willing to take?"

Sweet little Tina had an edge. And Ray had the pasty-faced, panicked look of a man who'd just figured out that he'd screwed with the wrong woman. "Fine, take your stuff and leave, but I better never see you sneaking around here again."

"Agreed." Tina turned to Ty. "I am so ready to get out of here."

Ty opened the truck door for her, then got in the driver's side. Ray watched, beady eyes narrowed, as if he thought this was some kind of trick. Ty was a little disappointed he hadn't had the opportunity to teach Cousin Ray a lesson or two, but Tina had handled the situation with confidence and finesse. Ty was impressed—not that he'd ever been anything but when it came to her.

"I guess you're not afraid of him anymore," Ty said.

Tina smiled. "Yeah. I guess I just saw him for what he really is."

"A slimy worm?"

"Pathetic," she said. "Sadly pathetic. And he can't hurt me anymore."

He started the truck, and as he pulled away from the curb, Tina rolled down her window and yelled to Ray. "By the way, sorry about the window!"

* * *

Tina sat cross-legged on the hotel-room bed next to Ty, nibbling on the fries left from their room-service order, while he sifted through one of the boxes of photos.

After leaving her aunt's house, he had checked them into a hotel—in separate rooms—and since neither of them felt like going back out into the cold, they'd settled in her room and ordered dinner.

"Here's another one with Ray," he said, holding it up for her to see.

"Pitch it," she said, feeling far too much satisfaction as he crumpled the photo into a ball and lobbed it at the trash can across the room—and made the shot *again*. That was ten for ten—he wasn't human. "Aren't you tired of looking through those?"

He shrugged. "Not much else to do."

They'd already surfed the very limited cable channels and found nothing of interest, and neither had felt like renting a pay-per-view movie.

Tina set her plate on the bedside table, fell back against the pillow and closed her eyes. It felt so good to wear something other than jeans and sweatshirts. As soon as they'd gotten to the room, she'd slipped into the bathroom and changed into knit stretch pants and an oversized, worn flannel shirt. Her comfy clothes.

She stretched her arms over her head and yawned.

"If you're tired I could go back to my room," Ty said.

"I'm not tired. Just bored."

"We could go out."

She scrunched up her nose. "Too cold."

She felt the bed shift, sensed that he was closer. She opened her eyes and found him lying next to her on his side, propped up on one elbow, gazing down at her.

They had taken a very large step today and she was sure he would need time to adjust. Which is why she hadn't thought twice about him coming into her room. She figured they would watch a movie, as they usually did, or just sit and talk.

Maybe it was her imagination, but Ty did not have the look of a man who wanted to talk.

He brushed a lock of hair back from her face and tucked it behind her ear. "We could fool around."

Just like that, she felt giddy and excited, like a teenager on a first date. And it felt wonderful. Where his finger brushed her cheek, the skin began to tingle, and she couldn't stop looking at his mouth. Her chest felt heavy, too, and so did her eyelids. Good grief, all she had to do was think about touching him, or kissing him, and she was toast.

Be the responsible one, that pesky, rational inner voice reminded her. "Do you think that's a good idea?"

"If you don't want to…" he said, sounding so adorably uncertain she had to grin. How could he not know how much she wanted this? Too much—which is why she was inclined to say no. Even she had limits. When Ty kissed her, her brain had this nasty habit of shorting out.

"It's not that I don't want to. I'm just worried that we would be pushing it."

"I kissed you this afternoon and I was all right," he said. "Why should now be any different?"

It was different because they were in a hotel room. It made her feel less…accountable, maybe. Not to mention that they were lying in bed. "We made some good progress today. I just don't want to push too far too soon."

"Do you have the slightest clue how fantastic it felt to kiss you today? I felt so *normal*. I want to feel that again. I trust you not to let it go too far."

Well, she was glad someone trusted her. She sure as heck didn't trust herself. But telling him no might only do more damage. The last thing she wanted was for him to feel rejected. "Okay, but if you feel anxious at all, I want you to stop."

He nodded. "I'd like to do it a little differently this time."

"Different how?"

"I want to touch you."

"Like holding hands?"

"No, we do that all the time. And I've touched your face, your neck." As if he felt compelled to prove his point, he caressed her cheek with the pad of his thumb, stroked her throat with the tips of his fingers. Her heart nearly stopped beating.

"See, no problem," he said, his eyes dark and intense. He toyed with the top button on her shirt. "I'm going to undo a few of these, okay?"

"Okay," she agreed, surprised by the huskiness in her voice. She should have been nervous, or at least a little scared, but all she could think was, Yes! Do it! Take it all off!

With the flick of two fingers he popped one button free. And another. Her body felt warm and heavy and her skin tingled in anticipation. He hesitated for a second, then undid one more. Cool air caressed the tops of her breasts as he very gently nudged the sides of her shirt apart. Watching her face intently, he touched one finger to her skin, tracing the lace cup of her bra. Down the swell of one breast and up the other.

Her skin shivered under his touch and the tips of her breasts pulled so tight they began to ache.

He slipped his finger just beneath the fabric and repeated the action, coming daringly close to her nipples. She could see his pulse throbbing at the base of his neck, but his eyes were heavy-lidded and showed no sign of distress.

Every part of her begged for more.

"I don't know if I've ever touched a woman like this before," he said, and when she gave him a disbelieving look, he grinned. "Of course I've touched a woman's breast before, but it was just a step in the process. I don't think I really paid attention to how it feels. Do you know what I mean?"

She wasn't sure how you could touch someone and not know how it feels. "Not really."

"I have a process," he said, stroking his fingers over the hollow at the base of her throat. "An order that I do things. I think that I get so caught up in the process, in reaching the goal, that I don't stop to enjoy what I'm doing."

"What's the goal?"

He slipped a finger under her bra strap, pulling it and the shirt off her shoulder. "Sexual satisfaction."

"That's it?"

"What else is there?"

"What about intimacy? Connecting emotionally?"

"Definitely not part of the process," he said, drawing a finger across her collarbone.

"There's your problem," she said, her voice sounding deep and whispery. "You have to let yourself feel."

"I feel you." He lowered his head, pressed his lips to her exposed shoulder and her internal furnace went from simmer to boil. "You could be standing ten feet away and I'd still feel you."

She sighed and let her eyes drift closed. *"That,"* she said, "is intimacy."

He brushed his lips across the swell of one breast, then the other. "Do you feel me?"

In every fiber of her being. "You bet."

She felt the heat of his hand on her stomach and a moan slipped past her lips before she could stop it.

"I guess you do," he said, his voice rough with desire.

She opened her eyes and realized that at some point he'd unbuttoned her shirt the rest of the way and it lay open, exposing her from the waist up. He was good. She hadn't even felt him do it, or maybe she was just too turned-on to care.

For his sake she'd tried to keep her wits, so he wouldn't feel pressured. But as he stroked her belly, as his fingers brushed the underside of her breast, she was past pretending this wasn't affecting her, that she wasn't melting under the heat of his touch.

"Has a man ever touched you like this?" he asked.

She shook her head. His palm closed over her breast and she arched into his hand.

"I wish you could see yourself right now. Your skin is flushed and your lips are red. You look like you're in total ecstasy."

"That's because I am," she said. She curled her fingers into the comforter. It was the only way she could stop herself from touching him back.

He gazed down at her, wearing a look of absolute fascination. "I don't think I've ever made a woman look this way before."

Somehow she found that very hard to believe. Maybe he'd just never paid close enough attention.

"I want to keep touching you. But I also want to kiss

you. The problem is, I don't think I can handle both at the same time."

"To be honest, I don't think I can either," she said. That made him grin, and cooled the mood just enough to give her the strength to pull the sides of her shirt together and re-fasten the buttons. "You seem to have a fairly good grasp on the whole touching thing. Why don't we work on kissing for a while."

"Sounds like a plan."

She'd reached her limit on the touching, but kissing she was pretty sure she could handle.

His eyes drifted to her mouth, then he lowered his head and brushed his lips against hers—slow and sweet and gentle. Oh yeah, this was nice. This she could handle. But it didn't take long to realize, sweet and gentle wasn't his intention. They blew right past sweet and dove headfirst into hot, wet and passionate.

And she went up in flames all over again.

Ty leaned in his office door, watching Tina as she tapped away at the keyboard. She'd cleaned a building today, so her hair was up, exposing the long, graceful line of her neck. It took all his willpower not to sneak up behind her and take a nibble of that soft, sweetly scented skin. In the week and a half since their trip to Philadelphia, he hadn't been able to keep his hands off her. They'd had more than a few hot and heavy make-out sessions on the couch in her flat or his living room, and a lot of over-the-clothes, above-the-waist petting. And there were still evenings when all they did was cuddle up and watch a movie together.

In a way, those were the times he enjoyed most. They were just together. She was curled up beside him, her head tucked under his chin, his arms around her. Sometimes she fell asleep like that, her long dark lashes resting against her cheeks, her breathing soft and slow. She looked so peaceful, so beautiful, he could watch her for hours.

Their relationship had developed into something that was so much more than sex, more than friendship. He wasn't quite sure how to label it, which normally would annoy the hell out of him. But he was having such a good time with her, he didn't even care.

"Got it!" Tina jabbed her hand triumphantly in the air as the computer screen lit and the system icon flashed. "It was a virus, that's why it kept locking up on you."

He stepped behind her, resting his hands on her shoulders. "Where did you learn to fix a computer?"

"Some on-line computer courses, but mostly self-taught. When cyberspace is your only link to the outside world, you learn to keep your computer in good working order."

He rested his chin on the top of her head, watched her fingers fly across the keyboard in a blur. "How fast do you type?"

She shrugged, not missing a beat. "I don't know. I never timed myself."

"What software do you know?"

She rattled off a list—all programs he used in the office. It was a smack-yourself-in-the-forehead moment. He'd been in desperate need of an office manager and all this time the perfect candidate had been staring him in the face. He'd been putting her very marketable office skills to waste by hiring her as a cleaning lady. What had he been thinking?

"What do you know about running an office?" he

asked, kneading his thumbs into the muscles at the top of her shoulders.

Her fingers dropped from the keyboard and she breathed a soft, blissful sigh. "Not much. God, does that feel good."

"Would you like to learn?"

She tipped her head back to look up at him. "To be an office manager? Why?"

"As you've probably noticed, I don't have one. I could train you. It pays more."

"What about the cleaning?"

"The truth is, I have a company that does the majority of the cleaning. I only kept Mae's sister on for the smaller places because I knew she needed the extra cash." He grinned down at her. "And I only hired you because you cried."

She narrowed her eyes at him, which looked pretty funny upside down. "I don't know if I should punch you or kiss you."

He grinned. "Hey, I like it rough."

Her stern look dissolved into a smile and there was no way he couldn't kiss her. Her full pink lips were just too damned irresistible, the tilt of her head too welcoming to refuse.

He lowered his head, brushed his lips over hers, felt her fingers slipping through his hair. He loved the way she touched him, so softly, but with purpose. Everything about her was soft and warm and exciting. And she always seemed to know exactly what to do to make him hot. She didn't even have to touch him. All she had to do was look at him with those dark, exotic eyes and he wanted her so badly he ached with it. A sweet ache. A wonderful, non-threatening ache. The waiting had been both torturous and fantastic at the same time.

He touched the edge of her lip with his tongue and she opened up to him, inviting him in for a taste. Her mouth was hot and tangy and he felt as though he could eat her alive. It made him so crazy he heard bells.

Then someone cleared their throat rather loudly, and he realized the bells he'd heard weren't in his head. The outer door had opened.

He lifted his head, saw his mother standing there, arms folded, one penciled brow raised. And she didn't look happy.

"Hey, Mom."

His mother gave them a look that could have bored through a foot of solid concrete, and Tina's shoulders went rigid under his hands. She knew better than to pull the intimidation crap with him. Tina on the other hand was fair game.

He really should have expected this. She'd called at least a dozen times in the past two weeks, pumping him for information. The first three times he'd politely, yet firmly told her to butt out. When that hadn't worked, he'd stopped answering the phone when her number came up on the caller ID.

He gave Tina's shoulders a reassuring squeeze, then motioned behind him to his office. "Come on, Mom. Let's get this over with."

She brushed past him into the office, her nose in the air and Tina looked up at him apologetically, as if she thought this was somehow her fault.

"Give me five minutes, then we'll talk about the office manager position," he said, then stepped into his office, closing the door behind him.

The second it snapped shut his mother rounded on him. "What office manager position?"

He walked around his desk and sank down into his chair. "Have a seat, Mom."

"What position?" she repeated, hovering over his desk. "You're not actually thinking of letting her work *here?*"

He folded his arms over his chest and leaned back. "Yep."

"Tyler Phillip Douglas, what in God's name are you thinking?"

He knew she was pretty far gone when she used his full name, and reasoning with her at this point would be impossible. He could only sit back and ride it out until she'd gotten it out of her system.

"It's inappropriate enough that you're practically living with her. She's a child! What would people think if they walked into your office and saw the two of you in a compromising position?"

That I'm one lucky son-of-a-bitch, Ty wanted to say, but he didn't think his mother would appreciate the stab at humor.

"You don't find it coincidental that she had no job and no money and has now latched on to you? She has gold digger written all over her!"

He resisted the urge to roll his eyes. Not this again. It was just like his mother to think the entire world was after his money. If he hadn't heard that one a million times. There was no doubt, he'd met his share of gold diggers, and he could spot one a mile away. That wasn't Tina at all. "She needs a job, I have an opening. It's as simple as that."

"You're a successful man. You have to be wary of people with less than noble intentions. Sex can cloud a man's judgment."

Was she kidding? He wasn't a horny teenager, even though it sort of felt that way lately. Not to mention the fact that he wasn't sleeping with Tina—not that he didn't want to. If anyone had less than noble intentions here, it was him.

He got up from his chair, walked around his desk and gave his mother a hug. She meant well, she just had weird ideas sometimes. He took her by the shoulders and said firmly, so there was no mistaking how he felt, "Mom, I appreciate your concern. I really do. But who I might, or might not be having sex with is really none of your business. And you should know by now that I don't care what other people think."

Her face softened into something that almost resembled a smile. "You're a good man. I just don't want to see you hurt."

"I know you don't. And I can take care of myself." He sat on the edge of his desk, and, knowing exactly how to get his mother's mind on something other than his personal life, said, "I haven't talked to Em in a while. How are the wedding plans going?"

She let out a long-suffering sigh. "Your sister is going to be the death of me. Do you know that she wants a man for a maid of honor? A *man!* What will people think?"

She rattled on about wedding plans for another ten or fifteen minutes, until his eyes began to glaze over. When he was finally able to usher her out the door, Tina was no longer at her desk—or what would be her desk if she accepted the job—but there was a note taped to the monitor: See you at home.

Home.

The word had taken on an entirely new meaning

since Tina had come into his life. And he had to wonder, what would happen, what would his life be like, when she decided it was time to leave?

Ten

"*Tyler Phillip Douglas, what in God's name are you thinking?*" Tina mumbled to herself, repeatedly driving the meat pounder with a bit more force than necessary into the boneless veal chops on the cutting board.

Not that Tina disagreed with his mother. When she and Ty were in public, it was best they try to keep their relationship professional, so people didn't get the wrong idea. But when he looked at her with so much affection and longing, as if she was the center of the universe, she was helpless to tell him no. And she was ashamed of herself for letting it get out of hand. She was supposed to be the responsible one.

What she didn't appreciate, however, and didn't *deserve,* was the gold-digger comment.

"What did that meat do to deserve such a beating?"

At the unexpected voice, Tina let out a screech of surprise and the meat pounder slipped from her fingers. It landed with a thud on the kitchen floor a fraction of an inch from her big toe.

"You scared me to death," Tina said to the woman standing in the kitchen doorway—another female version of Ty, meaning it had to be his sister, Emily.

"I knocked. No one answered so I let myself in." She walked to the counter, towering over Tina, and gazed down at the cutting board, her long, pale-blond ponytail swishing over her shoulder. "What was that?"

Tina looked down at the mutilated chops, pounded to a pulp. "Veal. I guess I got a little carried away."

"Sorry to pop in on you unannounced. I just had to meet the woman who my mother approves of even less than me." She didn't have the same stunning good looks as her brother, but Emily was pretty in a natural, outdoorsy way. And while she wasn't what Tina would consider overtly feminine, she had an easy grace, a simple beauty, that was almost hypnotizing. And they sure did breed them tall in the Douglas family. In suede work boots, she stood close to six feet.

She thrust out her hand. "I'm Emily," she said. "Douglas family black sheep."

Tina took Emily's hand, nearly wincing at her firm grip. "Tina DeLuca," she said, then couldn't help adding, "Douglas family gold digger."

Emily laughed, a deep, pleasant sound that seemed to emanate from deep inside her. Everything about her was bold and dynamic—just like Ty. Though his was subtler.

"Good old Mom. Isn't she a treasure? I'd make an excuse for her obnoxiously appalling behavior, but frankly, I've yet to find one."

"So it's not just me?"

"I'm her daughter and my only redeeming quality is my fiancé."

Meaning Tina didn't have a shot in hell of winning the woman over—not that she'd ever want to. Or need to, for that matter. It wasn't as though she and Ty had any sort of future together.

"What my mother fails to recognize is that behind all that twisted steel and sex appeal lurks an intelligent guy. Ty could spot a gold digger a mile away. Which means you couldn't possibly be one."

Tina felt a flood of affection for Ty's sister. "I appreciate that."

"And I feel compelled to warn you that although my brother is a really good guy, he's more than a little relationship-shy. Lately he's been acting downright weird. But you're nothing like the women he usually hangs out with, which makes me believe he must see something really special in you."

Yep, she really liked Emily. "Thank you."

Emily selected an olive from the relish tray on the counter and popped it in her mouth. "And you're living with him, which he would *never* do."

"Oh, no. I don't live *here*. He's letting me stay in the flat over the garage until I can afford a place of my own. We're just good friends."

Emily shrugged and said, "Okay."

From the front room Tina heard the door open, and the jingle of Ty's keys. He appeared in the kitchen doorway a second later looking rosy-cheeked, windblown and adorable.

"Hi, Em," he said, shrugging out of his jacket and tossing it over a kitchen chair. "What are you doing here?"

"I came to meet Tina," she said offering her brother a cheek.

He gave her a smack of a kiss, then walked over to Tina, stood behind her and wrapped his arms loosely around her waist. He touched her this way all the time, but that he would do it in front of his sister stunned her. Then he shocked her even more thoroughly by leaning down and planting a kiss right on her mouth. It was by no means passionate, but it wasn't exactly friendly either.

"She's not harassing you, is she?" Ty asked.

"Who me?" Emily said innocently. "Hey, speaking of harassment, have you thought about what I asked you?"

"What did you ask me?"

"The wedding?" she said sounding exasperated.

"Oh, that. Damn, Em. I don't know. Is he going to wear a dress?"

"He's gay, Tyler! Not a cross-dresser. He'll be wearing a tuxedo."

Tina looked back and forth between them, one eyebrow raised.

"She wants her maid of honor to be a guy, and I'm the best man. Which means we would have to walk down the aisle together."

"That's…different." Tina said.

"I don't have to touch him, do I?" Ty asked Emily.

"Nope, just walk side by side."

He thought about it for a minute, then grumbled, "Fine, I'll do it."

Emily smiled and popped another olive in her mouth. "I owe you."

"Big-time," he agreed.

"Matt has a game tonight. You guys should come."

"Her fiancé is the high-school football coach," Ty explained. "And we can't. Tina and I have plans."

Tina almost said, "we do?" then realized the nature of their "plans" and caught herself before the words slipped out.

"You are going to be there next Friday for homecoming?" Emily voiced it more like a demand than a question, and Tina detected the tiniest trace of her mother lurking somewhere beneath the surface. A trait she was sure Emily would deny to the death.

"Want to go to a football game next Friday?" Ty asked Tina.

"Um, sure."

"Seven o'clock," Emily said, then looked at her watch. "Damn, I'm gonna be late. Gotta go." She grabbed another olive and headed for the door, calling behind her. "Have fun, you two."

"She thinks something is going on between us," Tina said, after she heard the front door slam.

"Something is," he said, kissing her cheek.

"I like her. She's a lot like you."

"Sort of, I guess." His arms tightened around her waist, and he rested his chin on her shoulder. "You should have waited around the office. I would have given you a lift home."

"I needed some fresh air."

"Have you thought about the office manager position?"

Being with Ty, day in and day out. Honestly it sounded wonderful—if Tina didn't have to deal with his mother. How often did she stop in to see Ty, anyway? Weekly, daily? Did Tina need a constant reminder of how she didn't measure up? Of how temporary this arrangement would be? Would she only become more attached to Ty, all the while knowing it couldn't last?

The thought left a sick empty feeling in the pit of her stomach. Who was she kidding? She was *already* too attached.

"Okay," she said, telling herself it was for the extra money. So she could get her own place and start her own life. The longer she stayed here, the harder it would be to leave.

"Great. We'll start your training tomorrow." He looked over her shoulder at the cutting board. "What is that?"

"It *was* veal. I got a little overenthusiastic with the meat pounder."

"I guess."

"The gold-digger remark really stung."

Ty cringed. "You heard that, huh?"

"Your mom wasn't exactly using her indoor voice. Half the block probably heard."

"So you took out your frustration on a defenseless piece of beef?"

She laughed, but it came out sounding more like a sob, and tears welled up to the surface. What was wrong with her? It wasn't worth crying over.

Ty turned her in his arms, saw her face, swore softly, and pulled her tightly against him. "I'm sorry, Tina."

She rested her cheek against his shirt. His arms felt good around her—natural. It wasn't fair. It wasn't fair that she'd found a man this perfect, this wonderful, and they didn't have a chance in hell. "It's okay."

"No, it isn't. I'm so used to my mom, that kind of stuff goes in one ear and out the other. I know she's not saying it to be malicious. She's just a tad on the over-protective side."

"She's right about one thing. If you don't want people getting the wrong idea, you probably shouldn't kiss me in public. Or in front of your sister, for that matter."

"Why would I care what anyone thinks?" He held her at arm's length. "Or is it that *you* don't want people to know?"

She bit her lip.

"Tina?"

She shrugged. "I work for you, I live in your flat."

"So, what? Are you afraid people will think that I'm using you?"

"No! People would never think that. They love you. I don't want them to think that *I'm* using *you*. I have no idea how much money you make, but from the way your mother talks, I'm guessing it's a lot. People might think I'm after your money."

"That's my mother talking."

"Maybe she has a point."

"No, what she has is a serious case of paranoia, among other things. What I do in the privacy of my home, and with whom, is no one else's damn business. Do you feel like we're doing something immoral?"

"Of course not."

"Then what difference does it make what anyone else thinks?"

"It doesn't," she said, with more conviction than she actually felt. But if he didn't have a problem with it, she wasn't going to let it bother her either. At least, she'd try not to.

She looked over at the mutilated chops. "I think I murdered dinner."

He laughed. "If I ever make you mad, I'm going to hide that meat pounder."

She smiled up at him. He was so sweet and lovable and funny. Perfect—or darn close, anyway. "We could order out."

"Maybe later. I'm not hungry right now. Not for food anyway." He pulled her hair back, kissed the side of her neck. "Feel like fooling around?"

She loved the way he asked her that, the playful look in his eyes. "What did you have in mind?"

"My bedroom."

Yes! her inner voice shouted, but she forced herself to keep calm, to ask, "You're sure you're ready for that?"

"I am if you are."

She was so *very* ready. She felt him nibble her neck, felt his moist breath on her skin, and the edges of her mind went soft and fuzzy. Be rational, her mind taunted, be the responsible one. It's too fast.

And like the bad girl that she was lately, she told her rational self to stuff it.

Since that night in the hotel, they hadn't been near a bed. For the first time since then, Ty knew he was ready. He didn't even know how he knew. He just did. He took Tina's hand and led her out of the kitchen, up the stairs, and down the hall to his bedroom. A single, dim light burned on the table next to his bed.

"This is nice," she said, looking around, and he did the same, trying to see it through her eyes. He was neat by nature, so there were no dirty clothes on the floor or clutter lying around. The furniture was nothing exciting. Just a pine dresser and armoire and a king-size pine sleigh bed. The sheets were dark blue flannel with a plaid comforter to match. Basic guy stuff.

"I guess it's okay," he said.

"Big bed." She walked over to it and sat on the edge, bouncing a few times to test the springs. "Firm."

He crossed his arms across his chest. "You like things firm?"

One eyebrow lifted. "Sexual innuendos? This is new for us."

"I'd like to try a few new things tonight." He grabbed the hem of his shirt, pulled it up over his head, and tossed it on the foot of the bed.

"New is good." Her eyes got that heavy-lidded, dreamy look that he loved, the one that told him he was turning her on. He was well aware that this taking it slow business had been just as torturous for her. Women had needs, too, and this past week, all the touching he had done had to have been like one long tease. He was hoping that tonight he would be able to do something about that.

He walked over to the bed, to her.

"I know you've probably heard this a million times, but you have a beautiful body," she said, gazing at his chest. "You probably don't even work out."

"Three days a week for an hour. I go at lunch."

"Well, that's a relief. Because if you grew all of these muscles naturally, I would have to hate you."

He reached down and started unfastening the buttons on her shirt. With every button that popped loose, his body temperature rose ten degrees. He'd been waiting over a week for this night, to have his hands on her bare skin again, to feel her hands on him.

He slipped the shirt off her shoulders and down her arms and she tossed it aside. Her bra consisted of two triangles of pink silk and lace that barely contained the fullness of her breasts, but gave her a wonderfully deep cleft of cleavage. Her skin was smooth and dark and already flushed with desire. *Beautiful* didn't even begin to describe how amazing she looked. There were no words to explain the way he felt when he looked at her, or touched her. No words he knew of anyway.

Under normal circumstances, he'd have had the bra off her in seconds, but he was in no hurry. He was finding lately that the anticipation of the act was often just as exciting as the act itself. He liked taking his time, going slowly, stopping to notice every nuance of her skin, every dip and curve of her body. Some nights they kissed for an hour or more before he even got around to touching anything other than her face.

"Lie down," he said.

She scooted to the center of the bed, lying back against the pillows, watching expectantly as he kicked off his shoes and crawled in beside her. If she was nervous at all, she wasn't showing it.

"Is it okay to touch you?" she asked. "I don't want to push."

He took her hand and placed it on his chest. Her fingers were long and graceful, her skin cool and soft. "I want you to touch me. Just keep it above the waist. If it's too much, I'll stop you."

He leaned down to kiss her, nibbling her lips, teasing with the very tip of his tongue. While they kissed, she explored his chest with both hands, tentatively at first, as if she wasn't sure he could handle it, then more boldly. Still, he could feel her holding back, feel her restraint. She was trying really hard not to rush him, not to push him too far. Wouldn't she be in for a pleasant surprise?

He kissed her deeper, dipping into the sweetness of

her mouth, and felt her nails scrape across his skin. A week ago that would have done him in. He'd come a long way since then. He cupped her breast and she moaned, arching up against his hand. He wanted to make her moan, make her scream with pleasure.

He leaned back to watch her face. She looked like pure sex lying there, her cheeks and chest flushed with color, lips parted, her eyes half-closed. He traced the outermost edge of her bra with his finger, then repeated the action with the tip of his tongue.

Tina gasped his name and dug her nails into his shoulders. As much as he wanted to draw this out, he couldn't wait another second to look at her. He unfastened the front clasp on her bra and pushed it aside.

Perfect, just as he'd expected, and every part of him tightened with pleasure. Her breasts were full and round, the tips small and tight and the color of milk chocolate. There was something so exciting, so enticing about her coloring. The olive cast to her skin, the dark features. Maybe because she was so different from him. Whatever it was, he was in ecstasy just looking at her.

Through eyes that didn't want to stay open, Tina watched Ty watching her. He had a look of fascination on his face, as if he'd never seen bare breasts before. Which she knew for a fact he had, so why hers were so mesmerizing, she didn't have a clue. Then he lowered his head, touching her with his tongue, and he could have looked at her cross-eyed and it wouldn't have mattered. She groaned, sinking her fingers through his hair, feeling elated and aroused and miserable all at once. Because any minute now they were going to stop.

She ached to be touched. She was so hot, so damp

between her legs it hurt. She was sure if he didn't touch her soon, she would die from sexual frustration.

Through a haze she felt a tug at her waist and glancing down, saw that Ty was unsnapping her jeans, pulling the zipper down. For a second she was too bewildered to react. One part of her—the sexually tormented side—jumped up and screamed, do it!, while the other part said, in a substantially quieter tone, make him stop, it's too soon. He's not ready.

She tried to speak, but her voice cracked, so she cleared her throat and tried again. "Uh, Ty, what are you doing?"

He tugged her jeans down one hip. "Trying to take your pants off. And it isn't as easy as it looks, so you could give me a hand."

She considered arguing, then thought, nah, better to just play along. Wouldn't want him to feel dejected. That would definitely be bad.

She raised her rear end up so he could push her pants down, then kicked them off her feet. She lay there in her panties, more exposed than she'd ever been to another human being, thinking she should be a little nervous, or at the very least self-conscious. Instead she was on fire. Internal flames were burning her from the inside out.

Ty's face was flushed and his breath was coming faster, but if it was due to stress, she didn't know. She didn't *want* to know. She had to ask anyway, because he trusted her to stop him before it went too far. She *hated* being the responsible one. She swore, when he was over this and back to normal, she was never going to be responsible again in her whole life.

"Should we stop?" she asked.

"Do *you* want to stop?"

"No!" she said, a bit more enthusiastically than she'd intended, and he grinned.

"Then why don't you stop worrying about me, relax and enjoy this. Okay?"

She didn't need to be told twice. She closed her eyes and concentrated on the feeling of Ty exploring her body. He used his hands and his mouth and his teeth, with a tenderness that was downright torture, until she was out-of-her-mind excited.

"Have I told you how beautiful you are?" He stroked down her leg, across the sensitive skin of her inner thigh.

She couldn't answer—couldn't even think. She throbbed with need and desire. He was only making it worse—kissing her, touching her, as if he had all night. Come on, already, she wanted to say, but she was so far beyond verbalization it was ridiculous. She could barely even breathe. She could only whimper as his hands wandered lazily higher, up her thigh, drifted along the edge of her panties…over her stomach?

No, no, no. Other way. But he drifted higher still, up to her breast, through her hair. And all the while he kept kissing her senseless. She wanted to take his hand, put it where it was supposed to be, but she couldn't seem to make herself stop touching him. She let her hands wander across the steely planes of his smooth chest and stomach, the solid width of his shoulders, the sandy stubble on his chin. And his arms—how she loved his arms. So thick and sure. When they were around her, she felt as though nothing bad could touch her. Nothing in the world could hurt her.

His hands were wandering lower again. Driving her mad. Down…down, till he reached the top of her panties. He dallied there for a minute. The throb between her thighs was relentless now, painful even. She was so close, so ready…teetering right on the edge…just one little push…

Ty slipped his hand inside her panties, touched the slippery heat there. Her body rocked up against his hand and a strangled sound ripped from her throat. Then she flew apart, splintered into a million little pieces. In the back of her mind, all she could think was that she probably looked like those girls in the pictures she'd happened across on the Internet every now and then. Erotic pictures that had made her blush. She might have been embarrassed by her behavior if she didn't feel so amazingly, fantastically good. She felt like punching her fist in the air and screaming, YES!

When her vision cleared and she could focus again, she said breathlessly, "Oh, I needed that."

"It was fast."

"*Fast?* You call that fast?"

He grinned down at her. He knew darn well that didn't even resemble fast. "It was good?"

"Ty, that was better than good."

A wolfish grin curled his mouth and a mischievous gleam lit his eye. "Good, because we're going to do it again."

Eleven

"What is it?" Tina asked.

She and Ty stood side by side, foreheads nearly touching as they peered into the casserole dish at the brownish, greenish, gelatinous lump.

Ty's mother had been back. For the third time since Monday they'd come home from work to find a mystery dish in the refrigerator.

"I don't know." Ty grabbed a knife from the block and poked it a few times. "It appears to be dead."

"Is it…cooked?"

"It's hard to say. It looks kinda like cat food."

She elbowed him in the side. "That's mean."

He sniffed in the general direction of the dish, as if he were hesitant to get too close. "It smells like rotten eggs."

"Come on, it isn't *that* bad."

"So taste it."

She looked from him to the casserole, then shook her head. "No way."

"Why does she keep doing this? She knows you cook."

"That's probably why she's doing it." Because she wanted to pretend Tina didn't exist.

Ty's mother had stopped in the office to see him on Monday. She'd breezed right past Tina's desk, nose in the air, without acknowledging her existence. Same thing on Wednesday. It was as if Tina was invisible. Maybe Mrs. Douglas thought that if she ignored her, Tina would go away. And Tina couldn't decide which was worse, the hostility or the silence.

Since Tina had taken over running the office, it was at least clear why Ty's mother so ardently guarded her son's assets. There were, after all, so *many* of them.

As far as she could tell, he owned half of Chapel— houses, apartment buildings, offices and strip malls. Not to mention the countless properties in surrounding communities, and he had an entire building full of employees in a neighboring city to manage it all. He only went there a few hours a day, two or three days a week. The office in Chapel seemed to be his personal haven, and because he kept himself so separate from the heart of his business, she was under the distinct impression he didn't like the people in town knowing just how wealthy he was. It was the only explanation for his simple lifestyle when he had the resources to be living pretty high on the hog. Tina didn't know much about real estate, but with all the buildings he owned, he had to be worth millions. Maybe even tens of millions.

"Toss it," Ty said, giving the muck in the dish one final poke.

One more casserole bites the dust, she thought, trying not to let her delight show. It was petty of her, but she just couldn't help it. Ty's mother might have been a lot of things—wealthy and refined and sophisticated—but Tina would always be a better cook.

She held the dish over the sink, turning it upside-down, but the contents didn't budge. She gave it a shake, then pounded on the bottom. It wouldn't come loose.

"It's clinging on for dear life," Ty said, poking it a few more time to pry it loose. "Try it now."

Tina gave one more firm shake and the casserole came loose from the dish with a grotesque sucking noise and landed with a splat in the stainless-steel sink. Ty sawed it into pieces and stuffed it into the garbage disposal.

"This is ridiculous," he said. "I'm going to call her and tell her to stop doing this."

"Don't." As much as she disliked Ty's mother, Tina knew that Mrs. Douglas adored her son. She didn't deserve to get her feelings hurt for trying to take care of him, for being concerned about him. "She's probably a little jealous. She likes to take care of you, and I've honed in on her territory. If you tell her to stop sending food she'll be devastated."

Ty reached up, touched her cheek. There was such tenderness in the gesture her knees went weak. "You're amazing, you know that? My mother has been nothing but horrible to you, still you're worried about hurting her feelings. I don't understand how she can look at you and not see all the wonderful things that I do. How can she not know how special you are?"

Tina's heart filled with so much affection it felt as though it would burst. There was no doubt, she was one-hundred percent, head-over-heels in love with Ty. It was both horrible and wonderful. Because even if he could love her back, his mother would always hate her. And that would drive a wedge between him and his parents, and Tina couldn't live with the responsibility of that resting on her shoulders. She knew what it was like not to have a family. She was used to it. Even if she and Ty could make it work for a while, Ty would end up resenting her driving his family away. Even if he didn't mean to.

She couldn't live with that either.

Ty lowered his head, brushed his lips over hers, and her body responded instantly. She pushed aside all those unpleasant thoughts and lost herself in his kiss. It took only the slightest touch of his tongue to her lips and she opened up to him. There was nothing in the world like kissing Ty. And he couldn't seem to get enough of touching her, making her feel good.

Practically every night that week he'd taken her up to his bedroom, undressed her slowly, stripped her down to her panties. He always left them on. Probably one more step he hadn't been ready to take—until last night. Last night he'd knelt between her thighs and eased her panties down her legs, just looked at her for the longest time. Then he'd pressed her legs apart, leaned over and touched her with his mouth. It had been so intimate and forbidden, so personal, she had shattered almost instantly. He'd taken her hand and guided it to the front of his jeans. Even through the heavy denim she could tell that he was long and thick, and it probably would have been intimidating if she hadn't been so curious, so eager to touch him finally. But after only a few minutes he'd grabbed her hand.

"Not quite ready for that," he'd said, and though she'd been disappointed, she hadn't let it show.

Maybe tonight, she thought as Ty deepened the kiss, as he cupped her backside, pulling her against him, and she felt the ridge of his desire against her stomach. He was getting bolder, more comfortable with the idea of her touching him.

"Think we have time for a quickie?" he asked.

A *quickie? Quick* wasn't even a part of his vocabulary. There was nothing quick about the way he touched her. He liked to draw it out, make her crazy with desire. Then he would draw it out even longer.

Tina looked at the clock above the stove. "We're supposed to be at the game in fifteen minutes."

He cursed and let go of her. "I'd say, let's skip it, but Em called about ten times this week, asking if we still planned to go. I can't exactly back out now."

"It'll be fun," Tina said. "And when we get home, we have all night."

"All night, huh?" He gave her one of those smoldering looks, one that said very clearly that he would be holding her to it.

Tina knew even less about sports than she did real estate, but the citizens of Chapel took their football seriously, and she couldn't help getting caught up in the excitement. The bleachers were jammed with people, and hundreds more milled around the concession stand and behind the bleachers, making her wonder if the entire city was in attendance. According to Ty, if the team won this game, they would be in some sort of championship. Which, from the enthusiasm of the crowd, she figured was a pretty big deal. When the team scored a touchdown, putting them ahead by four points, everyone went wild. People screeched and clapped and blew obnoxiously loud horns. The marching band blasted out the fight song and cheerleaders hopped and flipped along the sidelines.

Sandwiched between Ty and Emily in the front row, Tina tried to follow what was happening on the field, but it was a little confusing. Ty shouted and whooped along with the crowd and Emily shouted encouragement to the players, addressing them all by name.

"This is Matt's first year coaching," she told Tina. "The kids just love him."

Tina hadn't met Emily's fiancé yet, but from what she understood he used to play professionally, and he had owned some sort of restaurant before he'd moved back to Chapel. And it was quite obvious that Emily adored him.

Something happened on the field and both Ty and Emily went wild, squishing her like a pancake. Ty sat close, his arm around her shoulder, a blanket draped over their legs to keep them warm. He seemed to know everyone. She'd met dozens of people, and thank goodness no one had greeted her with the same cool detachment as Mrs. Douglas. If anyone had their suspicions about her intentions, they'd kept it to themselves. In fact, a few people had seemed quite eager to meet her.

"Oh, *you're* Tina," they'd said. "Welcome to Chapel."

And then there were the people she'd met in the office this past week, and during their weekly trips to the grocery store. Everyone was just so friendly. They waved and smiled and said hello. A few stopped to chat. And everyone made it a point to educate her in the city's one claim to fame; the oldest chapel in the state of Michigan.

In the four weeks since she'd arrived, Chapel was starting to feel like home. She couldn't decide if that was a good or a bad thing. On the one hand, she would love to stay. But this thing with Ty was going to end, and staying in Chapel meant seeing him regularly. She wasn't sure if she could live in the same city with him, knowing they could never be together.

It would hurt too much.

"You okay?" Ty asked. "You have a funny look on your face."

She pasted on a smile. "I'm fine."

"You're bored silly, aren't you?"

"No, I'm having fun."

He leaned down and kissed her gently, in front of all those people. He tasted like chocolate and his nose was like an icicle.

He rubbed her shoulder. "Are you cold?"

"Nope. Toasty warm. But I think I'm going to go get a cup of hot cocoa. You want another one?"

"Sure."

"You want hot cocoa, Emily?"

"No thanks," Emily said distractedly, eyes glued to the field.

"You want me to come with you?" Ty asked.

"That's okay. I'll just be a minute."

Ty watched her walk away, until she disappeared into the crowd. He couldn't wait to get her home. He felt like a degenerate lately, unable to keep his hands off her, unable to stop thinking about getting her naked. She was so responsive to his every touch, so easily aroused. Giving her pleasure had been all the satisfaction he needed these past weeks. Although, when she'd touched him last night, stroked him through his jeans, he'd been in ecstasy. And he'd kept waiting for the anxiety to hit, for the fear to grip him.

It hadn't. He wasn't even sure why he'd stopped her. Maybe because he knew she'd never touched a man that way before, and he didn't want to scare her. Though she'd looked anything but scared. In all their time together, she'd never shown a hint of apprehension. If she hadn't come right out and told him she was inexperienced, he never would have guessed it.

Though his conscience was telling him to wait a while, that there was no rush, his body was saying, tonight. If he was ready to be touched, and Tina was ready to do the honors, why not? Tonight they would *both* get naked, and he would let her touch him, and he would touch her. And it would be amazing.

"I've never seen you so happy," Emily said, sliding beside him. "I've never seen you look at a woman the way you look at Tina."

"No?"

"No. But I think it's great. I think she's great."

Ty smiled. Thinking of Tina always brought a smile to his face—among other things. "She is. I love everything about her."

Em was silent, so he turned to look at her. She was staring at him, mouth agape. "*Love?* I don't think I've ever heard you say that about a woman, in *any* context."

He hadn't. He'd never been in love with anyone. Could this be what it felt like? Could this excited, content, life-is-freaking-wonderful feeling be love? Was that why he couldn't stop touching her, or stop thinking about touching her? Why he wanted to spend every minute of the day with her?

He tried to imagine what his life would be like without her in it and he honestly couldn't. What had he even done before she was there? It felt like a million years ago. And when he thought about spending the rest of his life with her, thought of marriage and babies and everything that went with it, it felt…*right*. All his life he'd said some day, when he met the right person, he would have all those things.

Was this his some day? Was Tina his right person?

"Tyler," Em said—slowly, deliberately. "Are you in love with her?"

"I think maybe I am."

She gave him a look, as if she expected him to laugh and say "just kidding." When he didn't, she said, "Holy cow, you're serious."

"I am. I'm in love with her." The words rolled naturally off his tongue, as if he'd been saying them his whole life.

He was in love with Tina. Who would have figured?

"The other day she told me you guys are just friends."

"Yeah, she's got this weird idea that people will think she's after me for my money."

"Gee, I wonder where she got that idea."

"Mom hasn't exactly been welcoming."

"She's been on a rampage about it. When I came to your house to meet Tina, I expected to find some bloodsucking, conniving vampire. I knew the second I saw her standing in the kitchen beating the hell out of those chops, she wasn't like that at all."

"She's not. I think my money actually makes her uncomfortable."

"She seems very…sweet."

"You say that like it's a bad thing."

"If she's going to make it in this family, she's going to have to learn not to take any crap. Being the perfect son that you are, you don't know how ruthless Mom can be. She'll pick and pick until she makes Tina's life miserable. She'll try to drive her away."

"It'll be fine," Ty said.

"I'm only telling you this so you know what to expect. I'm really happy for you. Surprised, but happy."

"I'm a bit surprised, too." Surprised that he'd been too big a dope to figure it out by himself. And Em was wrong. His mother would come around. Things would work out fine.

"You ready for another surprise?" Em asked. "You're going to be an uncle."

Ty laughed. "Since when?"

"I found out this week. I'm due in June."

"Well, damn." He gave her a hug. "Congratulations! I thought you didn't want kids right away."

"We didn't. This was a major oops. I thought we were being really careful. I guess you never know."

"Are you happy?"

"At first, when I was late, I felt like slitting my wrists. With the business just taking off I don't have time for a baby. I waited a whole month to take the test. I was in total denial. But Matt is so excited, it's hard not to be happy about it. He's already offered to be a stay-at-home dad if I want to keep working full-time."

"That's great, Em," he said, giving her a squeeze. "Have you told Mom and Dad?"

"I'm waiting until tomorrow at dinner. Mom is either going to freak out that I got knocked up before the wedding, or be totally ecstatic that she's finally getting a grandchild. You and Tina are coming, aren't you? I'm going to need all the moral support I can get."

He had completely forgotten about dinner at his parents'. Their monthly ritual. Maybe it would be the ideal time for them to get to know Tina. To see how wonderful she was. Once his mother got over feeling threatened or jealous, or whatever the heck it was that was making her act so weird, he knew she would fall in love with Tina.

Just as he had.

"Yeah, we'll be there," he said, then wondered how he could talk Tina into going with him. Maybe she didn't want to smooth things over with his mother. Maybe she didn't have the same feelings for him that he had for her.

What if he loved her, but she didn't love him back? What if she planned on leaving him eventually?

Emily slid away from him and he looked up to see that Tina had returned, holding two foam cups of hot cocoa. Her cheeks were rosy, her dark curls in disarray. She looked amazing. She looked like everything he could possibly want out of life. But did she see the same when she looked at him?

She handed him a cup and sat beside him. He covered her with the blanket and wrapped an arm over her shoulder. "What did I miss?"

If only she knew.

"First down, Chapel," Em said.

Tina snuggled close to him, all warmth and softness, resting her head on his shoulder. Her hair smelled of her apple shampoo and fresh air. He couldn't wait to touch her again. For her to touch him.

Definitely tonight, he decided.

He leaned close to her ear and whispered, "I just thought I'd warn you, so you have time to prepare, we're going to go home and finish what we started last night."

She didn't say a word. She didn't even look at him,

just smiled. Under the blanket, her hand came to rest on the uppermost part of his thigh and he went hard. That was all it took, all it ever took with Tina. She sat that way for several minutes, and try as he might, he couldn't concentrate on the game. Then her hand slid higher, under his coat and over his crotch, and he almost choked on his hot chocolate. If there was any question of exactly what she was and wasn't ready for, there was his answer.

She rubbed him through his jeans, not hard enough that any movement could be seen through the blanket— he checked—but hard enough to drive him crazy. To anyone watching, she appeared enthralled by the game. He on the other hand couldn't see straight. Probably had something to do with the lack of blood in his brain.

He couldn't believe she was touching him this way in the middle of a crowded stadium and he wasn't feeling an ounce of anxiety. And he was through waiting. They were going to go home and get naked. "We're leaving," he said, and Tina slipped her hand from his crotch.

"Right now?"

"Right now."

Twelve

"I can't believe I'm going to say this."

Tina closed her eyes, willing him not to say it. Wishing with everything in her that this time would be different. She'd really thought he would be okay. Up until that moment, everything had been perfect.

Ty had gotten them home in five minutes flat. They'd barely made it through the door before they were ripping each other's clothes off. They had tumbled naked into bed, kissing and touching. She was *finally* touching him. And because she'd thought this time was different, because she'd thought he was ready, she'd asked him to make love to her.

And he'd gone stone-still in her arms. She knew right then that she'd ruined it, still it didn't make it any easier to hear.

"I can't make love to you, Tina."

And there it was.

She took a deep breath, tried to calm her hammering heart. Tried to hide her disappointment. She was still lying in his arms, their legs entwined, their skin flushed and hot. It felt so right, so perfect. How could she have not sensed his anxiety? How could she have misjudged it so completely?

"It's okay," she said. "We'll give it a couple more days. Maybe you'll be ready then."

"No." He stared down at her, his face so open and honest—and full of regret. "I'm not saying I can't. I'm saying I won't. Making love was never part of the deal."

She was both relieved and confused. Did he think she didn't want to? Did he think he'd pushed *her* too far? "I really want to, Ty."

He rolled onto his back beside her. "So do I. That's the crazy part."

She propped herself up on one elbow. "But it's *really* okay."

"You say it's okay now, but what about later? What about a year from now? I just can't do that to you."

Later? A year from now? What was he talking about?

"It'll be fine then, too," she said, unable to mask the frustration in her voice. What did he want her to do, beg?

"Tina, we're talking about your first time."

"So?"

"I am lying here, ravaged by guilt, wondering how many first times I ruined. How many virgins did I have sex with because doing it with a virgin was like some kind of trophy? I took something precious from them, something they'll never get back." He looked over at her, his eyes filled with genuine concern. "I can't do that to you. I care too much about you."

His concern was admirable, but was he *kidding?* She appreciated the fact that he had an enormous amount of respect for her, but come on. She was a big girl, and more than capable of making her own decisions.

She sat up. "Ty, you're not stealing anything from me. I'm a grown woman, and I know exactly what I want. I'm giving it of my own free will."

He sat up beside her. "I still can't. Fooling around, making each other feel good, that's one thing. But making love. It's just too…special. Too personal. I won't have sex for the sake of having sex. It's not who I am anymore. Being with you has changed me."

"Well, change back, damn it!"

He shrugged. "I can't. I don't get it either. It's like, after twenty-eight years I've suddenly grown a conscience. This is so *not* me."

She felt like punching him. He wasn't going to budge. There was no way she could talk him into it. "I don't *believe* this."

He took her hands in his. "Tina, listen to me. When you make love to someone, it should be special."

"This *is* special."

He blew out a frustrated breath, as if she just wasn't getting it. "What I mean is, you should be in love."

"Don't you get it?" The words spilled out before she had a chance to stop them. "I'm in love with *you!*"

She cringed the second the words were out, when she saw the oh-no-what-have-I-done look on Ty's face. Way to go Tina. If he hadn't wanted to sleep with her before, he sure as hell wouldn't now.

He opened his mouth to speak, and she slapped a hand over it. "Don't. Don't talk until I've said what I have to say? All right?"

He nodded.

"I didn't mean to blurt that out," she said, her hand still over his mouth. "And I don't expect any kind of response from you. You don't have to love me back. And as far as making love, if you're worried that we're going to do it, that I'm going to expect more than you're willing to give, I won't. I have no illusions about our relationship. I know it would never work, and I'm okay with that. We'll just take this as far as we can, and hope we can still be good friends afterward."

He sat there, quietly watching her, so she continued. "I've been thinking about it a lot, and even though I didn't find my father, I might like to stay here. In Chapel," she added. "Not here, at your flat, because I'm going to have to find a place of my own eventually. I can't mooch off you forever. But I like it here. And it's not like I have anywhere else to go." She stopped and took a deep breath. "So, I guess what I'm saying is, I think I'll stay. Just so long as you know you're not under any obligation to me for anything."

He lifted her hand away from his mouth. "Are you done?"

"I think so."

"I can talk now?"

"Sure."

"Good." He leaned over and kissed her. "I love you, too."

"What?"

"I said, I love you, too. I would have said it before, but you wouldn't let me talk."

She sat there, astonished. He wasn't supposed to say that. He wasn't supposed to love her back. "But, you can't love me. We're all wrong for each other."

"Says who?"

"Your mother for one. She hates me."

Ty shrugged. "She'll get over it."

"It's not just that. You're too…" She waved her hands, searching for the right words. "*Perfect.* I mean, look at you. You're gorgeous and you have a wonderful body and you're sweet and considerate. We have fun together. You *respect* me."

He looked thoroughly amused. "So what you're saying is, I'm perfect for you, so I'm all wrong?"

"No…yes." She blew out a frustrated sigh. "I don't know. It sounds dumb when you say it like that."

"That's because it *is* dumb."

"I guess what I'm trying to say is, why would you want someone like me?"

"Why wouldn't I?"

"Because, I'm just…me. Nothing special."

He looked her thoroughly up and down, which was a little disconcerting considering she was naked. "You're special to me. You're intelligent and funny and beautiful and sexy and a thousand other little things all wrapped up that make you perfect for *me.*"

"Oh yeah," she said, pointing an accusing finger at him. "And you're rich."

He laughed. "This is different. A woman who *doesn't* want me for my money. I think I love you even more."

"Well, don't," she said. "Don't love me, because this relationship has failure written all over it."

"Too late. I already do."

"But you're not ready to settle down. You said so yourself."

"I also said, when I was ready to settle down, I would know it."

"But—"

He clasped a hand over her mouth. "Shut up, Tina."

He leaned over and kissed her. And kissed her…and kissed her. And because he did it so well, because she was drunk on the flavor of his mouth, lulled by the stroke of his tongue, she hardly felt herself falling back against the pillows. Then it was okay if he loved her, as long as he didn't stop touching her. *Never* stopped. And this time she was able to touch him back.

With curious hands she investigated all the secrets of his body and he did the same to her. As always, he took his time. A caress here, a nibble there, until her mind felt hazy and unfocused. He brought her to the farthest edge, half a step away from satisfaction, and held her, teetering there, until she thought she would go out of her mind from wanting him.

"Ty, make love to me," she said.

This time, instead of telling her no, he reached for the condom he'd left on the bedside table. She watched him tear it open and roll it on. He looked so large, and her own body seemed so small. She wondered vaguely if this was going to work. Wouldn't it be something if they'd come this far and discovered their bodies were completely incompatible? Could that even happen?

He knelt between her legs, lowered himself on top of her. She closed her eyes, clenched her fists. Please, please, she begged silently, let this work. She was scared and excited at the same time.

Ty pressed her thighs apart, stroking the damp skin there. "You're so beautiful," he murmured.

She held her breath when she felt him entering her.

He pushed, then nothing, then pushed again, but he didn't seem to be going anywhere. He wasn't inside her, it really *didn't* fit.

"Tina, relax," Ty said, and she opened her eyes, looked up at him.

"It doesn't fit," she said, feeling panicked. "I'm too small."

He grinned, not looking concerned at all. "It'll fit, you just need to loosen up a little. Unless you want me to stop."

"*No!* Don't stop." She unclenched her fists, tried to loosen up, tried to make herself go limp. Eyes locked on her face, Ty wrapped a hand around her hip, hiking her butt up in the air. With the slightest shift of his hips he was inside her, and she uttered a surprised little, "Oh!"

He drew back. "Does it hurt?"

"No," she said breathlessly. By all rights it should have, but it didn't. She couldn't even put into words what it felt like.

He pressed forward again, sinking deep…so deep. Just like that they were connected, their bodies interlocked. She realized she would never feel this whole again, this complete, unless Ty was making love to her. And he was right, it was so special, so personal and intimate, she couldn't imagine sharing this with anyone but him.

He held very still for a minute, then eased back out of her. She clutched his shoulders, arched up. "Don't stop."

"I won't." He thrust forward slowly, then back again, once then twice…then she stopped counting. Stopped thinking. He was kissing her, touching her, and she couldn't lie still, couldn't stop herself from moving against him. Her body took over, falling naturally in sync with his. She felt wanton and sexy, sank deeper and deeper into something hot and exciting. All that sensation, all that wonderful friction he was creating inside her pulsed slowly outward, swallowing her up from the inside out, making her mindless, spinning her out of control.

She was on the edge of something incredible, could feel her muscles tightening. Ty groaned and drove himself hard inside her and she shattered. She threw her head back, arched up against him as everything clenched, fast and hard and shocking, wrenching the energy from her body.

"Damn," Ty said and dropped his head on her shoulder, his thick arms caging her, his breath coming hard and fast. *"Damn."*

"Are you okay?" she asked, so limp she could barely push the words out.

He lifted his head, smiled down at her. "I am so much better than okay. I feel freaking wonderful. I feel normal…no, *better* than normal."

She smiled, feeling darned proud of herself. They had done it, they'd gotten Ty over his anxiety. He was cured.

"You know, I've had my share of sex, but I don't think I've ever really *felt* it. I didn't…I don't know… *connect*. Like, my head didn't feel what my body was feeling. Do you know I mean?"

"I think so."

"I don't know if it's because of what happened to me, or because I love you, or if I just wasn't paying attention before. But tonight, I felt *everything*. It was…oh, Tina, it was amazing. I wanted it to last, but then you started to come and I could feel it inside you. I can *still* feel it."

She smiled lazily. "Me, too."

"I didn't hurt you, did I? I wanted to go slower. I didn't mean to let it get out of hand."

"Did it get out of hand?"

"I feel like I ran a marathon." He rolled over on his back, pulling her across his chest.

She lay there feeling limp and lazy and wistful, his heart thudding against her ear. She could get used to this. She could imagine doing this for the rest of her life.

He stroked her back, the curve of her behind. "You're sure I didn't hurt you?"

She propped her chin on her chest, smiling up at him. "I'm sure."

"Still love me?"

"I still love you."

"Good. I'm going to tell you this now, while you're still feeling warm and fuzzy and your defenses are down."

"Uh-oh, that doesn't sound good. Tell me what?"

"We're going to my parents' for dinner tomorrow. And because you love me, you can't say no."

She narrowed her eyes at him. "Oh, that's rotten."

"I play dirty, I know."

"Does your mother know I'm coming?"

"I'm going to call in the morning and tell her." He stroked her cheek gently. "Please. Come to dinner. Give her a chance to get to know you."

He looked so sincere, and hopeful, and she couldn't tell him no, not when he looked at her that way. "Fine, I'll go."

He grinned and she melted inside. "I know when she gets to know you, she'll love you as much as I do."

She hoped he was right. Because if she didn't, Ty and Tina didn't stand a chance.

* * *

"Relax, it's going to be fine." Ty reached over and squeezed Tina's hand. It did nothing to ease the knots binding her stomach. The closer they got to his parents' house, the tighter they gripped. Deep down she just knew this was going to be a disaster, but she hadn't been able to back out of coming. She didn't want to let Ty down. She'd been seduced by his unwavering optimism. Somewhere between making love last night and waking in his arms this morning, she'd convinced herself they might have a shot.

Now she wasn't so sure.

She tucked her hair behind her ears, wishing it would, for once in her life, lie flat. She'd wrestled with it for an hour before finally giving up and letting it settle in its usual curly chaos. She'd spent almost as long in front of her closet, trying to decide what she wanted to wear. Ty said dinner was ultra-casual, meaning a dress was out, yet jeans felt too informal. She'd settled on a denim skirt that hung to mid calf, a cable-knit sweater, and flats. She'd even put on mascara and a touch of lip gloss.

Now that they were almost there, when there was no turning back, she was convinced her outfit was completely inappropriate.

She smoothed a hand over her skirt, a discount-store special, wondering if it looked cheap. "Maybe I should have worn something different."

"You look beautiful," Ty said. "Stop worrying."

"What if you're wrong and both your parents hate me?"

"They won't." He sounded so sure, so confident.

Then why did she feel this impending sense of doom? Why did she even care what Ty's parents thought of her? Ty loved her, that was all that mattered. At the very least, his parents would learn to tolerate her. Wouldn't they?

But is that how she wanted to live? Being tolerated? Always feeling second-rate? And if it caused a rift between Ty and his parents, that would be the worst.

He loved her, but love would only go so far. When it came down to him choosing between her or his family, whom would he pick?

It would never come down to that. She wouldn't allow it. She wouldn't let herself be responsible for tearing his family apart. She would leave first.

"I was thinking," Ty said, stroking his thumb over the top of her hand. "That maybe you should move some of your stuff into my house. So you don't have to keep running back and forth for things. In fact, maybe you should just move it all in."

Was he asking her to move in with him?

Tina was speechless for a full minute. She really didn't know what to say. It was true that lately she only went to the flat to sleep, and last night she hadn't even done that. But to move in with him? On the other hand, she'd been in Chapel a month and in all that time they'd been inseparable. Was a month long enough to get to know a person? To know if you were compatible enough to live together?

"It's a big step," she finally said.

"I know it is. And I want you to know that I've never asked a woman to move in with me. Hell, I've never even brought one home to meet my parents. Everything about us, about you and me together, feels right."

"What if dinner is a disaster and your parents both hate me?"

"They're not going to hate you," he said, and when she opened her mouth to object, he added, "But on the very slim chance that they don't accept this, taking you to meet them is only a formality as far as I'm concerned. I love you. I don't care what they think."

To hear him say it, to know he sincerely meant it, touched her somewhere deep down. And softened her up enough to say, "Yes, I'll move my stuff into your house."

He looked over at her and smiled. "As soon as we get home?"

"Sure," she agreed, which made this dinner that much more important. And made her that much more nervous.

Ty pulled down a street lined with picturesque maples and oaks all surging with brilliant reds and yellows and oranges, towering like sentinels around one enormous house after another. Figures they would live in a mansion. As if she wasn't intimidated enough.

"Here we are," Ty said, swinging into a circular drive and parking behind a black BMW and a forest-green pickup truck bearing a landscaping logo.

"Conway Landscape?" Tina asked.

"That's Emily's company," Ty said. "She probably came straight from work."

He shut off the engine and hopped out. She waited with increasing anxiety as he walked around to open her door.

"You ready?" he asked.

She shook her head. "Nope."

"It'll be fine. Trust me." He leaned in and kissed her, lightly at first, then a little deeper. Then deeper still, his hands caressing her face, slipping through her hair. And her apprehension started to slip just a little.

He was doing it again. Giving her hope. Making her think it might actually be okay.

"Hey, why don't you guys get a room?" someone called.

They pulled apart—Tina feeling a touch breathless—and looked over to see Emily standing in the open doorway, arms crossed, long blond hair tumbling all around her shoulders. "Are you planning on coming inside, or are you just going to sit out there and neck?"

"Do I have a choice?" Tina asked Ty.

He grinned and held out his hand. "It'll be fine."

He could say that a million times and she still would have a hard time believing him. She took his hand and hopped down, her knees feeling wobbly and soft, and they walked to the door together.

"Mom's in a mood," Emily said as they stepped up to the porch. "We got into it about the wedding this afternoon and her hackles are up. I thought I should warn you."

Tina's stomach pitched, and Ty gripped her hand tighter. "It'll be *fine.*"

He sounded confident, but there was something in his eyes that made her nervous, and had her wondering who he was trying to convince, her or himself.

Thirteen

Ty led Tina through the front door and she waited while he hung their jackets in the closet. The first thing that struck her was the absolute lack of color. Nearly everything was white. And not a warm, homey white either. It was a cold, sterile, don't-you-dare-touch-me-or-I'll-stain white. And all Tina could think was it had to be a bitch to keep it all clean.

The air smelled vaguely of bleach and some sort of meat. Not an appetizing combination.

"What's for dinner?" Ty asked Emily.

"Roast beef. At least, that's what she's calling it. Tina, would you like a glass of wine?"

God, yes, anything to take off the edge. "Please."

"Red okay?"

"Red is fine."

"One for me, too," Ty said, then turned to Tina. "I'll take you in to meet my dad and Matt."

He walked her through the house, over yards and yards of snow-white carpeting, past a winding staircase that led upstairs, and another that led down, until they reached the back of the house. French doors opened up to a monstrous deck and a solid wall of trees beyond. To the left was a white formal dining room, and to the right—big surprise, more white—the family room where two men sat, eyes glued to a gigantic flat-screen television.

"Michigan game," Ty told Tina, and raised his voice over the TV volume. "Matt, Dad, this is Tina."

Both men turned, and Tina was nearly blown backward by all the hard-bodied good looks and testosterone. Talk about hitting the gene-pool lottery. Ty's father, though definitely pushing sixty, had a thick head of salt-and-pepper hair, a lean, well-tuned physique and a striking, youthful face that she was guessing had seen its share of nips and tucks. Matt was just plain old gorgeous. The kind of man you looked at and sighed, and thought, *perfection.*

They both stood and Tina nearly got neck strain looking up at them. She could have worn six-inch heels and she would still feel like a midget around all these tall people.

"Tina." With a vague smile Mr. Douglas shook her hand—a wishy-washy, tip-of-the fingers shake—then he glanced distractedly back to the television. He was neither friendly, nor rude. Just sort of…disinterested.

Could be worse, she decided, as he reclaimed his seat. Anything was better than contempt.

Matt on the other hand greeted her with a friendly, knock-your-socks-off smile. He clasped her hand firmly, his dark eyes warm and inviting. "It's a pleasure to meet you, Tina."

She could see he meant it, and that took a hint of the pressure off. At least someone here wasn't predisposed to hating her guts. And though he was the picture of male perfection, she could see by his demeanor, by the casual way he carried himself, that he didn't have a pretentious bone in his body. A high-school football coach was definitely more her speed. And what had Emily said? Her fiancé was her only redeeming quality, which meant her parents must really approve. If they approved of a coach, maybe they would get used to Tina, too.

This was good. She finally felt she had some sort of ally. Someone she could relate to. And maybe someone who could give her pointers in the best way to deal with Ty's parents.

This was very, *very* good.

"Dinner is almost ready," Emily said, stepping into the room with two glasses of wine. She handed them to Tina and Ty, then turned to Matt. "Honey, did you tell Ty about the villa?"

"Oh, yeah, it finally sold," Matt said. "My realtor called yesterday."

"I told you it would go fast," Ty said sipping his wine. "It's a sellers' market. How'd you make out?"

"We made a decent profit," Matt said, and turned to Emily. "What did we figure, honey?"

Tina took a sip of her wine—

"About eight million, I think."

—and promptly choked on it.

Eight million? They were talking dollars, right?

Ty rubbed her back as she hacked and coughed. "Hey, you okay?"

Tina nodded, eyes tearing as the full-bodied wine burned a path into her lungs. "Went down the wrong tube," she croaked.

"My carpet!" someone screeched, and everyone turned to see Mrs. Douglas standing behind them, apron knotted around her waist, glaring at Tina.

Then all eyes were suddenly focused on the floor. Tina looked down, cringing when she saw that her wine had sloshed over, leaving a crimson stain on the pristine carpet.

Wonderful. Ty's mother had probably been hiding around the corner, just waiting for Tina to do something wrong, to make a mistake, so she could pounce.

"Sorry," Tina wheezed.

"It's ruined!"

"It's Stainmaster for God sakes," Emily mumbled, rolling her eyes. She turned to her mother. "Don't worry, I'll clean it up."

Ty took Tina's glass, passing it off to Matt, and thumped her on the back. Mrs. Douglas let out a long-suffering sigh, swiping at an invisible wisp of hair at her forehead. "Dinner is ready."

And with that, the evening went from bad to worse.

God-awful.

It was the only way to describe Mrs. Douglas's cooking. The roast was desert-dry, as if it had been cooked three or four hours longer than necessary, the gravy was almost as thick and lumpy as the tasteless mashed potatoes and had even less flavor. In contrast, the broccoli was so undercooked it was crunchy and swimming in over-salted gooey cheese sauce.

It was a culinary nightmare.

But Tina ate it, because it would have been rude not to. Every so often Ty would look over at her and smile sympathetically, rub a hand over her back or touch her arm. But for the most part Tina had been invisible, save for a few malevolent looks from his mother. She listened to them all talk, gleaning, among other things, that not only was Matt a football coach, but he had recently sold a profitable restaurant chain and probably had more money than everyone else at the table combined. Meaning she'd lost her only ally.

Ty's mother, Tina soon realized, had an almost pathological need to keep everyone's attention centered on herself. She had a comment about everything said, and manipulated every conversation so it inevitably revolved around her.

Emily mentioned having had to fire an employee for insubordination. She felt awful about it, but the girl just wouldn't do things Emily's way. That's nothing, Mrs. Douglas said. She'd fired a whole slew of housekeepers who wouldn't clean to her specifications. Finally she'd given up completely on hired help and—insert long-suffering sigh—decided it was easier to do it herself.

Ty mentioned a difficult tenant, a man who was consistently a month behind on the rent.

"A month?" His mother had said. "That's all? Remember that place on Fourth Street we used to own, the law office? That tenant was a nightmare. We felt lucky if we were paid at all. A lawyer for heaven's sake and he couldn't even pay the rent on time! Remember that, Phil?"

Ty's father nodded, uttering a vague sound of agreement.

"And the mess he left when we finally evicted him. It's why we sold our properties." She exhaled another sigh with an eye-roll added for emphasis. "We had so many horrible tenants. Everyone is out to take advantage of you." She shot Tina a meaningful look, as if to include her in that elite group. And since Tina favored being ignored over the rude jabs any day, she tried to make herself invisible. She just sat quietly and watched, listened to the conversation. As long as she could remain invisible, she had a chance of making it out of there in one piece.

"So, Tina," Matt said. "How do you like Chapel?"

All eyes were suddenly on her, and Tina cringed inwardly. She knew he was only trying to be polite, trying to include her in the conversation. She forced a smile.

"I like it," she said. "Everyone has been really nice."

She glanced up at Mrs. Douglas and wished she had the guts to add, "almost everyone." But she knew being confrontational wouldn't help. No matter how much Mrs. Douglas deserved it.

"Where are you from?" Emily asked.

"Philadelphia," she said.

"Originally?" Mrs. Douglas said, as if she'd expected an altogether different answer, like Mars. Or at the very least, somewhere south of the border. Is that what this was about? Tina's ethnic origins?

"Philly born and raised." Tina forced herself to take another bite of rubbery, unchewable meat, washing it down whole with a gulp of wine, thinking, *God, get me out of here.*

"Quality wine is so much better sipped," Mrs. Douglas said, lifting her glass and demonstrating. "We always let Matthew choose the wine." She reached across the table and patted Matt's arm. "He has impeccable taste. We just adore him."

Matt flashed Mrs. Douglas a strained smile.

There was an invisible, "And despise you," tacked on the end of that sentence. Pitting Tina against Matt, that was an interesting twist. She took another swig of her wine, not giving a damn how slowly she was supposed to drink it. Ty sat quietly beside her, eating his food, shoulders tense.

"Ty tells us you're an amazing cook," Emily said to Tina. "We're expecting an invitation to dinner."

"Is your mother a cook as well?" Mrs. Douglas asked. Another veiled jab, although the veil was getting mighty thin.

"My mother was a waitress," Tina said. "She passed away when I was six."

"Your father," Mrs. Douglas said. "What does he do?"

And the questions just kept getting better. Tina took another guzzle of wine, draining her glass. Liquid strength. Because she knew what was coming next. And Ty, savior that he was, automatically refilled her glass. That's right, keep it coming. "I never knew my father."

"He passed away, too?" Mrs. Douglas inquired. She almost sounded friendly, but Tina knew she was digging for information—for ammo. And she was about to get what she wanted.

"I don't know," Tina said. "He and my mother never married."

"Oh, so you're illegitimate?" Mrs. Douglas said it casually, as if she were just making pleasant conversation. Tina noticed Ty's knuckles go white around the fork he clutched and he shot his mother a look. A look she ignored.

Tina took another swallow of wine. It was that or spring over the table and strangle Ty's mother. Someone needed to put a leash on that woman—preferably one with a muzzle attached.

"So Tina, what are your long-term plans?" she asked, obviously on a roll now. "Will you leave Chapel when Tyler no longer requires your…*services?*"

Services?

Didn't have to be a rocket scientist to know what she meant by that one. All around the table, mouths fell open. Even Ty's father rejoined the land of the living long enough to look surprised by his wife's insinuation.

Tina just felt like crawling under the table and hiding.

Ty looked like any second his head would explode. But he turned to his mother, smiled and said, calm as you please, "Tina's not leaving Chapel. In fact, she's moving in with me."

It was almost worth the look of utter indignation on Mrs. Douglas's face. "Don't you think that's inappropriate?"

Ty looked his mother square in the eyes and said through gritted teeth. "As a matter of fact, I don't."

A long uncomfortable silence ensued, as if no one was quite sure what to say.

"We're pregnant," Matt blurted out, taking the focus off Ty and Tina, serving himself up as sacrificial lamb. "I just thought everyone would like to know."

"You're what?" Mrs. Douglas's mouth gaped open. "But, you're not married yet. It's bad enough you're living together. What will people think?"

"Oh, brother." Emily groaned and dropped her head in her hands. And even though Tina's head was already feeling fuzzy, she took another drink of wine. No way would she make it through this evening sober.

Ty's mother looked from Emily to Matt, then to Ty

and Tina, and screeched, "What is happening to this family?"

Ty slammed his fork down onto the table and everyone, including his mother, jumped. From their stunned expressions, Tina was guessing Ty didn't lose his cool very often.

He pushed back his chair and rose to his feet. "A word, Mother?"

Mrs. Douglas took her napkin from her lap and threw it on her plate, following her son out of the room in a huff.

Tina realized it was the first time she'd ever seen Ty so angry. Even after the pepper-spray incident he hadn't looked this upset. And it was all her fault.

"So," Mr. Douglas said, turning to Emily and Matt, as if nothing was out of the ordinary. "When is the baby due?"

Ty led his mother into his dad's study and shut the door behind them. He'd been patient, had given her the benefit of the doubt, but this time she'd pushed too far. It was one thing to be overbearing and judgmental—everyone was used to that. Tonight she'd been downright vicious.

This was his own fault. She'd been horrible for weeks, and instead of facing the problem head-on, he'd ignored it in the hopes that it would go away. Just as Tina said, he lacked coping skills, and damn it, he didn't like to make waves.

He should have set her straight that first day.

"What was that out there?" he asked. "The Spanish Inquisition?"

His mother crossed her arms over her chest, chin lifted defiantly. "This was *your* idea. You *had* to bring her here. You *wanted* me to get to know her. Well, she doesn't talk. How can I be expected to get to know her without asking questions?"

"Questions that belittle and insult her?"

"Such as?"

"Don't play dumb. You know exactly what you were insinuating. *Everyone* knew."

"If she has nothing to hide, why should she take offense to anything I ask? Maybe you just don't like hearing the truth."

"You still think she's after my money?"

"I can't believe that you don't! She's already weaseled her way into your home."

"She hasn't weaseled her way anywhere. I asked her to move in. She was afraid to get involved *because* of my money."

"I'm sure that's what she wants you to think. And then you know what will happen? She'll wind up *pregnant*. Then what would you do?"

That was a no-brainer. It's not like he wasn't going to ask her eventually anyway. In fact, he wouldn't mind at all if she turned up pregnant. "Marry her," he said.

His mother looked horrified. It would have been entertaining if not for her next words. "You would do no such thing, not if you intend to remain a member of this family."

Ty's blood ran cold, and because he was sure he must have misheard her, that she couldn't possibly mean what she'd just said, he asked, "I beg your pardon?"

"I won't have it. It's one thing to have a fling with a girl like that, but marriage? That is completely unacceptable."

Anger, hot and intense, pulsed at his temples. "A girl like *what,* Mom?"

She huffed out a breath. "A tramp! That's what. I mean, look at her. She's obviously not like us."

"Not *like* us?" he said. "And what exactly is that supposed to mean?"

She pressed her lips into a firm line, refusing to answer, but he knew damn well what she meant and it sickened him.

"What are we talking about?" he asked, aware that he was getting louder, and realized by her taken-aback expression that it was the first time he'd ever raised his voice to her. It was the first time she'd ever deserved it. "Is it social class? Ethnicity? She's different because her skin is a little darker than mine? Does that make her a lower-class citizen? Unworthy of my love?"

She didn't deny it. She only stood there looking stubborn and self-righteous. And he could feel his blood pressure rising.

He forced himself to stay calm, to be reasonable. "If you can't bring yourself to like Tina, fine. I'll have to live with that. But I expect you to treat her with respect, and I want you to apologize for your behavior tonight."

She looked scandalized by the mere idea. "I will do no such thing."

"Fine. Have it your way." If she wouldn't give an inch, neither would he. And he had to end this conversation, before he said something he would regret.

"Thank you for dinner." He opened the door and walked back to the dining room. He heard hushed conversation, but everyone stopped talking when he entered the room.

Tina sat stony-faced, her face devoid of emotion, but he knew she was hurt. What person wouldn't be?

"She means well," his father said. "She's just been under a lot of stress lately."

"I don't care how much stress she's been under," Ty said. "There is no excuse for the way she acted. Tina, we're leaving."

Fourteen

Ty peeled out of his parents' driveway, feeling angrier and more frustrated than he had in his whole damned life. He knew his mother could be narrow-minded and judgmental, but this was over the top even for her.

"I'm really, really sorry," Tina said.

"*You're* sorry? What the hell for?"

"For everything that happened in there. It was a disaster."

"And how was that your fault?"

She closed her eyes and leaned her head back against the headrest. It was almost dark, but he could see she was close to tears. "By just being alive, I think."

"Tina, listen to me. What happened in there had nothing to do with you and everything to do with my mother being a self-righteous snob. I'm the one who's sorry.

I shouldn't have let her treat you like that. But I can promise you, it won't happen again."

"If you changed your mind, I understand."

"Changed my mind about what?"

"About me moving in."

He gripped the steering wheel tighter. "I did *not* change my mind."

"Maybe it would be better if I didn't."

"Tina, I want you in my life. In my house. If that means not seeing my mother, fine. I can live with that."

"This is what I was afraid would happen," she said, shaking her head. "You have no idea what it's like not to have family. You say you can live with not seeing her, but you're going to cool off and start to think rationally and you'll realize you can't do that. You and your mom are close. I can't compete with that. I wouldn't even want to."

"No one is asking you to."

"If our relationship comes between your relationship with your mother, you're going to resent me for it. Maybe not right away, but somewhere down the road you will."

She didn't get it. She wasn't the bad guy here. And he'd be damned if he was going to give up the one woman in his life he had ever loved just because his mother had some over-inflated superiority complex. "Tina, the only person I resent right now is my mother. End of story."

They were silent the rest of the way home. When they got there she waited while he walked around and opened her door.

"I'm going to go up to my flat and change." She stepped down out of the truck, losing her balance as she landed on the pavement.

He caught her arm. "You okay?"

She gave her head a little shake, as if to clear it. "Yeah, just a little woozy from the wine, I think. It didn't really hit me till we were driving home."

"You only had two glasses."

"That's two more than I usually have."

"I'll walk you up." The last thing he needed was her falling down the stairs. And he had the sneaking suspicion that once she got into her flat, she wouldn't be coming back out. She was probably still blaming herself, and feeling guilty, and would tell him she wanted to be alone.

Though he expected an argument, she nodded and let him lead her up the stairs and into the flat. A single lamp beside the couch shed pale light throughout the room. He'd barely gotten the door closed when she wove her arms around his neck, got up on her tiptoes and kissed him.

Okay, maybe she didn't want to be alone. After what she'd been through, he'd been sure sex would be the furthest thing from her mind.

"Make love to me, Ty," she murmured against his mouth, shoving his jacket off his shoulders.

Or not.

And, hey, that was okay, too. Her absolute abandon, total trust, still got to him sometimes. It made him realize how precious this relationship was, and just how much he had to lose if he screwed it up.

She gasped as he lifted her off her feet and carried her to the bedroom, setting her down beside the bed. She wasted no time shedding her jacket and sweater and tugged her skirt off. The entire rotten evening drifted somewhere into the back of his mind as he watched her undress. Watched her unfasten her bra, her breasts spilling out, tempting him. He wondered if she had any idea how much he wanted her, how different their relationship was from anything he'd ever experienced. He could tell her a million times, and he still didn't think she would ever understand. Hell, he didn't even understand it.

He pulled off his shirt, and by the time he unfastened his jeans, Tina was naked and kneeling on the unmade bed waiting for him. What limited inhibitions she might have had, which weren't many to begin with, had apparently been canceled out by the wine. She looked like pure sex kneeling there, and nothing like a recently deflowered virgin.

He shoved his pants down, kicking them away.

"Come here," she said, motioning to him with a crooked finger, a lusty smile on her face. "I want to try something different."

"Different, huh?" He liked the sound of that, having uttered it more than a few times himself in the past month. He walked to the bed and Tina wrapped her arms around his neck, her body soft and warm against him as they kissed. She tasted like wine and femininity, like everything he could possibly ever want in a woman.

She trailed kisses down his chin, his throat. She ran her tongue across one nipple, then the other, then bit them lightly, making him shiver. She kissed lower still—down his stomach, stopping to swirl her tongue in his navel, and everything below his waist pulsed in ecstasy. Then she wrapped a hand around the length of him, lowered her head, and took him in her mouth.

He groaned and closed his eyes, sliding his fingers through her hair. Her mouth was so hot, the sensation so out-of-this world fantastic, his knees nearly gave out.

Then she cupped him between his legs—almost hesitantly as if she thought she might hurt him. Then she became bolder, exploring lower still. A moan ripped from his throat, and his fingers tangled in her hair.

He knew, two more minutes and it would be over. He wanted to make love to her, wanted to be inside her.

She made a noise of protest as he lifted her up and half-laid, half-tossed her onto her back. She looked up at him, lids heavy, lips damp as he lowered himself on top of her. Her legs instantly encircled his waist and he could see, this wasn't going to be slow, sweet lovemaking.

She was slick and hot and the intense sensations he experienced as he entered her seared him inside and out. A growl rumbled from his throat and Tina cried out with him. He pulled back and plunged forward again, felt his eyes roll up. It had been fantastic last night, but this was off the charts. Then it hit him, he wasn't wearing a condom. That's why it felt so damn good. He didn't even have any with him. They were back in the house.

He honestly thought about stopping—for about a half a second. He tried to make himself consider the consequences. What he could be getting himself into. A vision of her body rounded and full, carrying his child, flashed across his mind, and instead of sending him into a panic, he pumped faster, harder. Primal need canceled out the last of his good sense until he no longer cared about the risks. He wanted to make her his. Whatever it took.

And by then it was too late, because Tina arched up, crying out as her body clamped down hard around him. Then he couldn't stop. His own release was fast and furious, and left him slumped against her, gasping for air. They were both slick with perspiration, a sweaty tangle of arms and legs.

They lay quietly for several minutes, then Tina asked softly, "We didn't use any protection, did we?"

Damn. He was hoping maybe she hadn't noticed. "No, we didn't."

"Was that accidental?"

He cursed and shook his head. "I could have stopped. I didn't *want* to stop."

She sighed. "You can't make her accept me by knocking me up. In fact, me suddenly turning up pregnant will look awfully suspicious at this point, don't you think?"

He lifted his head and looked at her. She didn't look angry, just…resigned. "Tina, I'm sorry. I wasn't thinking. I never stopped to think that you wouldn't even want—"

She caught his face in her hands. "I would love to have a baby with you someday. You know I want a family. But with everything else we have going against us right now, it's probably not the time."

"You're right. I'm sorry. I was being selfish."

"I don't think we have anything to worry about. I'm due to start my period any minute now."

"That's good," he said, telling himself he should be feeling relief, when instead disappointment curled through him.

"Maybe, for the future, I should think about going on the pill or something."

"However you want to handle it," he said. He was in no position to try to make any more decisions for her.

He rolled onto his back and Tina curled up against his side, reaching down for the blankets and covering them waist high.

"I love you," she said, and he gave her a squeeze.

"I love hearing you say that."

"I just hope it's enough. Us loving each other, I mean."

"If you're talking about the situation with my mother, I know it will work out. I really believe that once she has time to cool down and think about what I said to her tonight, she'll come around. Maybe you guys will never be pals, but you can at least find some balance and learn to coexist without killing each other."

"I can't go through life letting her walk all over me."

"You won't have to." He held her tighter, kissed the top of her head. "Everything will work out."

It *had* to. He loved her so much, he could no longer imagine his life without her in it.

Ty was so engrossed with the images on his computer screen that when his office door slammed shut, he jumped a mile. He looked up to see his sister standing over his desk.

More like hovering really. It amazed him at times how much she looked and acted like their mother. Of course, if he ever told her that, she would probably break his nose.

"Christ, Em, you scared the hell out of me."

"Where is Tina?"

"She went to the bank to drop off a deposit."

"Good, because we need to talk. You have to help me!"

"Help you with what?" he asked.

"You have to apologize to Mom, before she drives me crazy. She's been like my shadow lately."

"Apologize for *what?* She's the one being unreasonable. She thinks she can boss me around and I'll just blindly do what she says."

"Welcome to my life. How do you think she's been treating me the past twenty-eight years? I couldn't do anything right!"

"Then you should be happy."

"This is even worse. Now that she's mad at you, she's smothering me! She's been calling me at work, bringing food over. It's like she suddenly wants to be my best friend."

"Yeah, well, welcome to *my* life."

"Ty, it's been two weeks. Can't you at least try to patch things up? She actually called me up in tears this morning, saying you don't love her anymore."

"Why should I be the one to try to patch things up when I haven't done anything wrong?" He felt bad that his mother was upset—which is exactly what she wanted. It's how she always managed to get her way. Till now. He was tired of playing that game. If he gave in, nothing would ever change.

"Look, Em, I hate this. I hate confrontation. I'm not very good at it. And it makes me sick to know that I'm making Mom unhappy…"

"So talk to her, Ty!"

"…but I can't live my life by her standards."

Emily tossed her hands up in defeat. "You're both impossibly stubborn."

"All I'm asking for is an apology for the way she treated Tina, and a promise that in the future she'll treat her with respect. That isn't much to ask for."

"For Mom it is."

"Take a look at this," Ty said, pointing to his computer screen. Emily walked around his desk, mouth gaping when she saw the Internet page he was looking at.

"Those are engagement rings."

"Yeah, but I'm pretty much clueless about jewelry. What do you think? Two, three carats?"

"Men and their preoccupation with size," Emily said, shaking her head. "I don't see Tina as the type to be impressed by an enormous rock. I'd go for something unique."

"An exotic-looking stone," Ty said. "Something with a little color."

"Exactly."

"How much time do you have?"

Em looked at her watch. "An hour maybe."

Ty got up and grabbed his jacket. "Let's go shopping."

Tina started in the direction of home, the brisk wind snapping at her cheeks. It was nothing compared to the deep ache that had settled in her heart. After coming back to the office from the bank and overhearing Ty and Emily talking—a conversation never intended for her ears—it had become clear this situation was far worse than she'd realized. Ty's mother was miserable, and he was, too. And it was all Tina's fault. When he said it made him sick that he was hurting his mother, that was all Tina could bear to hear.

Though Ty had tried hard not to let it show, he'd grown increasingly cranky and upset over the past two weeks, evidence that this situation with his mother was bugging him more than he wanted to admit. And it would only get worse. Any time now he would begin to resent Tina—if he didn't already.

This was proof that two people could be in love, and still be all wrong for each other. She should have known this was too good to be true. Men like Ty didn't fit with girls like her. It had been destined to fail from the beginning, although she couldn't honestly say she would have done things any differently. She'd been able to help him, and he'd helped her get back on her feet. Their relationship had been mutually beneficial.

Now even Ty couldn't deny it would be best if they called it quits.

It might be a while before she could afford her own place, and until then she would move her things back into the flat. She would also have to try to find another job. If they were going to make a clean break, it would be better if she wasn't in his house cooking him meals, or in the office with him every day. Maybe Mae would consider hiring her as a cook and she could pay Ty rent until she found another apartment.

Or maybe she should leave Chapel altogether.

She looked around at this city that had become so familiar: the coffee shop that made the best caramel lattes— Ty's favorite—and Mae's Diner where she and Ty often had lunch. The grocery store where she and Ty shopped together every week. The bank where she dropped deposits and had opened her first savings account.

Nearly every building, every place she'd been to, was attached to a memory of Ty.

"Miss DeLuca?"

Tina turned to see Mr. Lopez walking up the sidewalk toward her. Even though she knew he wasn't her father, that it couldn't be possible, there was something there, a feeling when she looked at him. And the empty space in her heart, the longing for a real family, only intensified.

"I was wondering if we could talk," he said. "Could I buy you a cup of coffee?"

"Now isn't a very good time for me."

"I feel really bad for the way things happened when you came by my house. I thought we could talk about it."

The last thing she needed was to sit and have coffee

with this man. A reminder of what she didn't have—what she would *never* have. As it was, she was barely holding it together. "No offense, Mr. Lopez, but I don't want to talk to you."

"You might when you hear what I have to say."

Something in his tone, the look in his eyes, raised the hair on the back of her neck. "What could we possibly have to talk about?"

"The fact that I lied to you."

Fifteen

Tina sat across from Mr. Lopez—Marty, as he'd asked her to call him—in a booth at Mae's, stirring a packet of sugar into her cup. She was only going through the motions. Her stomach was so tied in knots she didn't think she'd be able to choke it down. "So, what you're saying is, you did spend the weekend with my mother?"

"Yes, I did." He had the decency to look guilty for lying to her.

"So it's possible that you are, in fact, my father."

"I would say the likelihood is high. You look just like my daughter, Lucy. I thought so that night."

Still, he hadn't told her the truth. She didn't know which was worse, not knowing who her father was, or being rejected by him. "In other words, you knew then, but you didn't want to accept responsibility."

"I don't blame you for being angry and hurt. And

you're going to like me even less when I tell you why I lied. I was married when I spent the weekend with your mother."

Wow, it just keeps getting better, she thought. "I take it your wife didn't know about it?"

"Not up until a few weeks ago."

Well, that at least explained why he'd lied. So his wife wouldn't find out. It was better than him lying because he just didn't want to have anything to do with her. Though, that part could be coming next.

"I loved my wife very much, I still do. She's my soul mate. But when I met your mother, she was so passionate, so full of life. We were drawn to each other instantly."

"Did she know you were married?"

"She did. That first night in the diner, we talked for hours. What happened between us just…happened. Neither of us expected it, or planned it.

"I finally told my wife last week. But she said she'd figured it out the minute she saw you. She kept waiting for me to say something, to tell her the truth. I didn't want to hurt her. I didn't want to hurt you either. I didn't know what to do. I hope you can understand the position I was in."

"I never meant to put you in that position. I guess I never stopped to think about how it would affect your family." All the searching, all the waiting, for nothing. She'd been so focused on herself, she hadn't stopped to think what she would be doing to his family. When she'd thought she couldn't feel any lonelier, any emptier, it just kept getting worse.

"I know you meant well."

"I don't want to cause you any more trouble," she

said, her voice unsteady. "I realize it will be difficult to avoid each other completely, but I'll do my best to stay away from your family from now on."

"That would be a shame, because my wife is very interested in getting to know you, and introducing you to Lucy. Your sister." He reached across the table and slipped a hand over one of her own. "I'd like the chance to get to know you, Tina. Would you let me do that?"

Suddenly everything she'd ever wanted, ever dreamed of, was right in front of her.

"I'd like that," she said, tears brimming in her eyes. "I'd like that a lot."

"Tina! You home?" Ty shut the front door and shrugged out of his jacket, tossing it over the arm of the sofa in the front room. She hadn't come back to the office after her trip to the bank, and he'd called the house half a dozen times trying to get hold of her. Now he was downright worried.

He walked through the house to the kitchen. "Tina, you here?"

"Right here." She emerged from the laundry room behind the kitchen, a basket of clothes in her arms, and he went weak with relief. Until he saw the look on her face. "Tina, what happened? You look upset. Have you been crying?"

She avoided his eyes. "It's been an eventful day. I have a lot to tell you."

He followed her through the house and up the stairs to the bedroom, growing increasingly uneasy. Then he saw two of his suitcases lying open on the bed, and he knew something was really wrong. "What is this?"

"I'm borrowing them. As soon as I get my things moved, I'll bring them back."

"Get your things moved where?" he asked, suddenly feeling panicked. Had it been his mother? Had she gotten to Tina again? "Tina, what's going on?"

Tina began folding the clothes from the basket and placing them neatly in the smaller of the two suitcases. "Martin Lopez came to see me today."

"What for?"

"To tell me he lied to me. He really is my father."

"Why did he lie?"

"He was married when he slept with my mom. But he's talked to his wife and his daughter about it, and they've forgiven him. They want me to be a part of their family. I spent most of the afternoon with him at Mae's, just talking and getting to know each other."

"That's fantastic, Tina. So why don't you look happy?"

She wouldn't look at him as she spoke. "My half-sister, Lucy, lives in Royal Oak. I guess it's not too far from here."

"I know where it is."

"Well, she has an apartment above the lingerie shop she manages and she's looking for a roommate. The owner of the shop just had a baby, and she thinks I can probably work there for a while."

He could hear what she was saying, but for some reason it wasn't sinking in. "You have a job. And a place to live."

"I think we both know that isn't working out."

"Of course it is. You're the best office manager I've ever had."

She kept her eyes lowered. "You know that's not what I mean."

What was she talking about? He'd never been happier in his life. He yanked the basket away from her. "Damn it, Tina, look at me."

She looked up at him, her eyes brimming with tears. "You're miserable, your mother is miserable. I think it would be best if I just go."

"First off, I am *not* miserable. And what does my mother being miserable have to do with me and you? If she's unhappy, that's her own damn problem, not mine."

"You haven't been yourself lately. You can't deny this thing with your mother is bothering you."

"Of course it's bothering me, but not enough to end our relationship. That is what we're talking about, right? About ending this?"

"You said it makes you sick that you're hurting her. Well, it's only going to get worse Ty. She's never going to accept me."

He spat out a curse. "You heard me and Em talking?"

She lowered her head, and nodded.

"I'll say it again, for the thousandth time. *I don't care what my mother thinks.*"

Tina looked up at him, her eyes cold. "Maybe you should."

"Meaning what?"

"Has it ever occurred to you that your mother is right? That I've been using you?"

"In fact, no, it hasn't."

"Maybe I only told you I loved you to get you to sleep with me. Maybe getting you into bed was a challenge for me. A project. Maybe the sex wasn't even that good."

"The sex was damned good," he said.

"For you maybe. But us con artists are pretty good at faking it." Tina fought to keep her tone, her face, devoid of emotion, when inside, she was falling apart. Her hands shook and her knees wobbled. Why wouldn't he just let her leave? Why couldn't he see it was for the best? Why was he making her do this? She didn't want to hurt him, but if that was the only way to make him listen, it's what she would have to do. "You don't think it's a coincidence that the second I find a way out of your life I'm taking it?"

He stared at her, knuckles white where he clutched the laundry basket. Finally, he said, "If that's the way you want to play this, fine. Give me a holler when you're done and I'll carry the suitcases down for you."

He tossed the basket back down on the bed and walked out of the room.

It was what she wanted, but instead of feeling relieved, she just felt sick inside. Maybe she hadn't expected him to give up so easily. Maybe she'd wanted him to fight for her.

No, it was better this way.

On unsteady legs, she walked to the bathroom and stuffed her toiletries into a plastic grocery bag. This was a good thing. It would give her time to get to know her family, to start fresh. Again.

Tina dumped the last of the clothes on the bed, folding them with trembling fingers and packing them in the suitcase. The worst part about all of this was knowing that she was hurting Ty. But he had a close family and dozens of friends. He would be over her in no time. Then he would probably look back and wonder what it was he ever saw in her. He would find a nice, acceptable woman to marry and his mother would be happy. Everyone would be happy.

"Are you ready?"

Tina looked up to see Ty standing in the bedroom doorway, face stoic. He didn't look too broken up about her leaving.

Maybe he was over her already.

She stuffed the last shirt in without folding it, and zipped both suitcases shut. Her fingers shook so badly the tab kept slipping from her grasp and it took her several tries to get them both closed. She was so close to a meltdown. She had to get out of there. She couldn't let him know how devastated she was.

She pushed her shoulders back and drew a last morsel of strength from somewhere deep inside. "Ready."

"Do you want a ride, or should I call a cab?"

No way she would be able to sit with him in his truck while he drove her away from the place she'd so desperately hoped to make her home. She still wanted to. "I think a cab would be better."

He walked over to her and every one of her nerve endings pulsed with awareness. She would be able to do this as long as he didn't touch her. If he tried to hold her, or kiss her, she would break down.

But he didn't touch her. He hefted the suitcases off the bed as if they were weightless, and said, "Let's go."

She followed him out of the bedroom and down the stairs, clutching the banister to give herself balance. With each step, her hands shook harder, her heart beat faster. She was really going to do this. She was going to pretend she didn't love him, that this wasn't destroying her, and she was going to walk out the door.

Her head began to spin and her skin felt clammy. She felt surreal, as if she were being sucked into a vacuum. When she hit the bottom step and saw Ty's parents sitting on the sofa in the front room, for a second, she thought she was hallucinating. "Wh—what are they doing here?"

Ty set the suitcases down and said, "Hey, if you can play dirty, so can I."

"I'd like to know what we're doing here as well," his mother said, her voice huffy and full of contempt. Ty's father sat beside her, a half smile on his face, looking as though he knew exactly what was going on and he was enjoying himself thoroughly. Did he hate her now, too?

Did Ty plan to torture her? Was this her punishment for leaving him?

"I had Dad bring you here, so you could see what you've done," Ty said to his mother. "You've been trying like hell to drive Tina away, and here she is, her bags packed. Are you happy?"

Surprisingly, his mother didn't seem to take too much satisfaction from that news. Tina thought she'd be off the couch cheering.

"I also brought you here to ask you a question. What is it about me you find so unlovable that Tina couldn't possibly be in love with me?"

"I—I don't find you unlovable at all," his mother stammered. "How could you even think such a thing?"

"So then, it's Tina? She's the one with the problem."

Her eyes darkened and she glared at Tina. "You know exactly how I feel about that."

"Okay, tell me why you feel that way. What has she done, besides being the victim of some pretty rotten circumstances, that you find so offensive."

Here it comes, Tina thought. A laundry list of why she wasn't right for her son. This would be torture. But Ty's mother didn't say anything.

"Has she been rude to you?" Ty asked.

She paused, as if trying to conjure up some instance where Tina had been anything but polite. Finally, she said, "No."

"Has she been rude to Dad?"

"Nope," Ty's dad said pleasantly. "I like her."

His wife shot him a look of irritation.

"Did she steal from your house? Maybe run off with the silverware after dinner?"

"Not that I'm aware of," his mother said.

"So, what did she do?"

"I'm worried that she's using you," she said, as if that was a given.

"For what? My money? Any money I've given her, she's worked for. She cooks in exchange for rent because she refuses to take a handout. I've offered to buy her stuff, she never lets me. She's never asked me for a damn thing. So where exactly do you get the idea she's using me? Where is the proof?"

Mrs. Douglas didn't answer.

"I'm assuming by your lack of response, that you have no proof. That you dislike Tina just because you feel like it."

"I'm trying to protect you," Mrs. Douglas said. "I just want you to be happy."

"Do you really?"

"Of course! That's all I've ever wanted for you and Emily."

"On whose terms? Because I am happy with Tina. I'm in love with her. When I think about the future, I can't even imagine her not in it. Do you understand that I have never felt this way about a woman before? And she loves me so much, she was going to walk away because you don't approve of her. Because she thinks my

relationship with her is going to break our family apart."
He turned to Tina. "But I'm not letting her go."

This hadn't been about torturing her. All this time he
was trying to make her stay. Tears burned in the corners
of Tina's eyes. She loved him so much it hurt. A good hurt.

"The truth is," Ty told his mother. "you probably
wouldn't like or trust anyone I brought home to meet
you, because that's the kind of person you are. And despite that, I love you. But I won't have it anymore. I never should have let it go as far as I did."

"Maybe I was unduly harsh," his mother conceded.
"I'm very protective when it comes to my children."

"I'm not asking much. I'm not asking you to be
Tina's best friend. You don't have to be her friend at all.
I do however expect you to be respectful to her. Can you
do that?"

After a pause, his mother nodded. She didn't look
one-hundred percent thrilled with the idea, but she
didn't look hostile either. It was a start.

"Tina, you have a say in this, too. Can you live with
that?" Ty asked.

Live with it? It was more than she'd ever expected.
"I can live with that."

"So we're agreed?" Ty said, and both women nodded their heads. "Good. Now, I was going to wait until
we were alone to do this, but what the hell." He pulled
a small velvet-covered jewelry box out of his pants
pocket and flipped it open. Inside was a ring; an irides-
cent stone set in a delicate band of braided gold and sil-
ver. A ring so beautiful it took her breath away.

"The second I saw it, I knew it was exactly what I
wanted to get you," he said. "I hope you don't mind that
it isn't a diamond."

It could have been a chunk of glass and she would have loved it all the same because it was from him. And if he felt the need to prove he loved her, he didn't have to buy her anything. She was already convinced.

Then he dropped down on one knee in front of her and Tina's breath caught in her throat. He wasn't just giving her jewelry, he was *proposing!*

He looked up at her and grinned and said simply, "Marry me?"

"Absolutely." He took her hand and slipped the ring on her finger. It was a perfect fit.

They were a perfect fit.

Forgetting they had an audience, she threw her arms around Ty's neck and kissed him.

"You didn't really think I would let you leave, did you?" he whispered, and she hugged him even harder. "This is it for me. You're my someday."

She cupped his face in her hands, in awe that this amazing man loved her that much. "This is real, isn't it? I'm not imagining this."

"So real that I don't want to wait to get married."

"I don't want to wait either."

"And nothing big. In fact, why don't we just go next week to a justice of the peace."

"Tyler Phillip Douglas!" his mother shrieked, looking aghast. "You will do no such thing!"

Ty's father rolled his eyes and shook his head.

"You're having a *real* wedding," she said sternly. "And we'll need at least six months to plan."

"Six months?" Ty asked.

"You wouldn't deny your mother the privilege of attending her only son's wedding?"

Ty looked at Tina questioningly.

She shrugged. "I don't mind."

"Okay," Ty told his mother. "But I mean it when I say nothing too big."

Tina looked from Ty to his parents. "I don't really know anything about planning a wedding."

Mrs. Douglas gave a what-would-the-world-do-without-me sigh. "Well, thank goodness I know exactly what you'll need. We'll have to start planning right away."

"Okay," Tina agreed, wondering exactly what she was getting herself into, but considering it a small price to pay if it kept a sense of unity in place. Maybe they could even learn to like each other a little.

She also got the feeling this was no accident.

"Why don't we meet for lunch tomorrow at the house?"

"Lunch tomorrow will be fine."

Ty's dad got up, pulling his wife with him. "We should go," he said. "Congratulations you two."

"Think about your colors," Mrs. Douglas said as her husband ushered her out the door. "Lunch is at twelve sharp!"

The door shut behind them, and Ty wrapped his arms around her.

She looked up at him. "You never really wanted to get married at the justice of the peace, did you?"

He only grinned.

"You knew the idea would drive her nuts, and she would want to plan the wedding. And in doing so, she and I would have to interact."

His grin widened.

"Very sneaky."

"If there's one thing my mother excels at, it's planning parties. She'll only drive you a little crazy. But I promise, I'll never let her hurt you again. I won't let *any-one* hurt you."

"I know you won't."

"It may take a while to get all the gears running smoothly."

"I'd say we're off to a pretty good start."

He framed her face in his hands, kissing her gently. "I can't imagine where I would be right now if I'd never met you. You've made me a better man."

"And you've given me the one thing I've always wanted the most," she said. "A family."

* * * * *

Coming in June 2005
from Silhouette Desire

Emilie Rose's
SCANDALOUS PASSION

(Silhouette Desire #1660)

Phoebe Drew feared intimate photos
of her and her first love, Carter Jones,
would jeopardize her grandfather's
political career. So she went to Carter
for help finding them. But digging up
the past also uncovered long-hidden
passion, leaving Phoebe to wonder if
falling for Carter again would prove
to be her most scandalous decision.

*Available at your
favorite retail outlet.*